WEDDING VOWS & MURDER

A Violet Carlyle Historical Mystery

BETH BYERS

SUMMARY

April 1925.

Violet and Jack are finally getting married! The date has been saved, the flowers have been bought, and the baker is working on a creation of layers upon layers. With all of the parties and teas to satisfy Violet's stepmother, no one could be more ready for the wedding day to arrive than these two.

When, however, Vi and Jack find a body at one of the pre-wedding parties, they expect their wedding plans to be a little askew. Only the victim is someone they both despised. Now Violet and Jack must solve the murder before their joyful day is ruined. Will they be able to solve the crime, say their vows, and get on with their lives? Or is their happily ever after ruined?

CHAPTER ONE

"Why did you want to wait?" Violet asked, crossing her hands over Jack's chest and propping her chin on top of them. It was a very early April morning and their wedding was mere days away. And—they were still sleeping with the bedroom door open to protect her virtue.

To say she was glad they were so close to their wedding day was to say she was glad the house hadn't burst into flames and that everyone hadn't been struck down with the measles. She wasn't sure that she wanted anything more than to marry him and shut that bedroom door. She grinned at the door for a moment and then turned her mischievous gaze on her beloved. "Are you really that afraid of my father?"

Jack had a bit of scruff on his face, and his penetrating gaze took in her face. He knew her smirk too well, and his face smoothed into his own even expression that hid his feelings. "I suppose we're notorious enough."

He grinned at her—one of those rare things that only she ever got to see. A defenseless, honest expression appeared on his face and he sat up, pulling her with him so she was kneeling over his legs.

It was moments like that when she had to acknowledge just how large and strong Jack was, and comparing him to a mountain would not be amiss. He had a strong jaw and broad shoulders that begged her burdens. He wasn't the most handsome of men, but he called to something within Vi.

She was smart enough to know that it was because he wanted her for *who* she was. Not *what* she was. Not the heiress. Not the earl's daughter. Not the remnant of some old family that claimed privileges by birth and the accomplishments of those long dead.

He simply wanted Violet, and he knew what that meant. She was devoted, loving, interfering, clever, educated, prone towards the blues, a friend to be counted on and just as likely to spend an afternoon ensuring orphaned children had what they needed as to spend the day in bed with a stack of ridiculous novels and a pot of coffee.

She was witty enough to be the one her great aunt left her fortune to. It wasn't favoritism that had Vi as the recipient. It was because Violet had learned how to manage and invest the money. As clever as she was, she wrote pulp novels for the sheer joy of an absurd piece of fiction.

Jack nuzzled her with his whisker-covered chin. "Nothing is more important to me than you and your happiness. Maybe you'd have regretted making love before we married. If we had an early baby, basic mathematics aren't all that hard for a child later. Is it so hard to wait? Is it so hard to avoid having to tell a child we were living as if we were married before we were? Our friends won't care, Vi, but our society hasn't changed all that much. Don't we have the rest of our lives to enjoy that aspect of being together? Without everyone else's judgement and commentary?"

Violet was tempted to place a blistering kiss on him, but the temptation to go beyond mere kisses had been growing stronger and stronger than she'd have thought possible. It was getting so difficult to remain chaste that they barely touched when they were awake. She'd have thought Jack would have abandoned sleeping with her if not for her nightmares.

There was so much to be happy about at the moment despite her dreams. Victor and Kate had found a country house a mere five minutes motoring from Jack's country home. Violet's stepmother, Lady

Eleanor, had turned her unwanted attention to her own daughter when Isolde had eloped.

Their wedding had fallen together, and all that was left was the baking of the cake and the arrival of the day. Vi and Jack's house was even finished.

The paper had been hung on the walls, the furniture they'd ordered had arrived, the floors had been refinished, and as a gift, Jack had the great hall ceiling painted, along with the bedroom that would have been the lady of the house's if they hadn't intended to share one. Instead, it was part office, part boudoir, part personal library. It was painted with the night sky, with the merest shadow of dragons worked into the darkness, so one could only identify them if they knew to look for them. To say she loved her gift wasn't enough, and she was eager to finally move into their home, even when it meant leaving her twin's house, though that was only down the street.

Instead of kissing him as she wanted to, she leaned into his chest, breathed him in twice, and then swung off the bed, winked, and skipped into the bathroom, her dog, Rouge, following, yipping in excitement.

Victor and Kate were already in the breakfast room when Violet arrived. Vi leaned down and pressed a kiss on Kate's cheek, letting her hand pass over the baby growing in her sister-in-law. "How is my baby?"

"I think you mean my baby." Victor stood when Violet arrived and crossed to the buffet to pour a cup of her favorite Turkish coffee. The twins had the same love for Turkish coffee that matched all the other corresponding points between them. Despite being fraternal twins, they had the same slim builds, the same witty gazes, the same dark hair and eyes. They were, to put it simply, two sides of the same coin.

"No." Violet turned to her twin. "I am certain I mean mine."

Victor handed over the cup to his sister before pressing his own kiss on Kate just over where Vi had left one. "Father will murder us all if there is an actual baby for you, pretty devil," he told Vi.

"No worries on that score, Victor darling." With a more serious tone, she asked, "Did you read the end of the book?"

"I did. I read. I winced. I envisioned the reaction when Lady Eleanor discovers there is a Lady Léonor, part-witch, part-goblin, in the book. You're still planning on having the heroine, a sweet young but clever woman, be forced to burn the stepmother and monster alive?"

"Something must be done," Violet told him. "If this is what it takes to make her stop bothering Jack? I think I shall hand-deliver it to her with an offer to change the woman's name to something different... perhaps Hester...but only with a solemn promise to simply allow me the fate I have created. For good or ill. She must leave Jack alone."

Victor shook his head. "My sweet, dear demon. You are tempting the bear to attack."

"It *is* a challenge," Kate finished. "If you let Lady Eleanor escape, perhaps she will leave you alone."

Violet grinned at her sister-in-law. Kate and Victor had been married a few short weeks less than they'd been expecting a baby, prompting the earl's threats to both of his daughters' beloveds. For Isolde and Tomas—they had eloped, escaped to the Caribbean, and returned only to pull the focus of Isolde's mother and furious father away from Vi. For Vi—she and Jack had been towing the virtuous line.

Towing that line did not, however, equal living a fantasy where Lady Eleanor stopped interfering in their lives. Nothing had stopped her before, but now Violet was no longer willing to put on a polite face.

"Are you going to the party this evening?" Victor asked Violet as Jack entered the room, shaved and crisp with his hair slicked back.

Sliding his pocket watch into its home, Jack took and refilled Violet's coffee and then made his own. He made a second trip to the buffet, retiring to the table with two plates. Vi glanced down at the one he'd made for her. It was piled high with kedgeree, toast, bacon, sausages, and tomatoes. She stared at Jack, who didn't seem to notice her look while he overloaded his toast with marmalade.

Violet didn't believe for a second that Jack didn't notice her expression, but he was ignoring her. She shoveled half the food to the side and started with a bite of the fried tomatoes before setting her fork down to sigh into her perfect coffee again. "Yes, of course, we're going. Algie is engaged to an American heiress. I *must* meet her. Is she marrying him for his connection to the nobility? It is rather distant. Does she love him? He's such a...ah..."

"Daft fool?" Victor suggested.

"Easy mark?" Kate added with a bit of a delicate wince, as though she felt bad for saying such things. Violet lifted a brow and Kate rubbed her stomach. "I suppose his mother thought he was lovely."

"Lovable idiot," Violet finished, staring at Kate for her remark. "Are you afraid Violet Junior is going to be a fool like Algie?" she asked.

Kate flinched and glanced away.

"Not possible." Violet resolutely set down her coffee and leaned forward to emphasize her statement. "Dearest Kate, perhaps if only Victor were involved here, but with your brains? Let alone mine! Little Vi will be fine. A bit too clever for her own good, perhaps."

"Certainly," Jack added, and then slightly pushed Violet's plate closer to her.

"What is this?" Vi demanded, nudging the plate back.

"You're thinner."

"I'm getting married," Violet told him. "Every girl under the sun worries about her looks before her marriage. Except Kate. As she was sicking up into the bin."

Kate scowled at Violet, but she agreed with her a moment later in sisterly solidarity. "She's right."

"There's nothing wrong with your figure," Victor choked out. "Has she gone mad?"

"She's always been vain," Kate told him. "Women are extra vain around their wedding days. It's a special kind of science."

"Vain?" Violet gasped, holding her throat.

"Any woman with as much makeup and as many stuffed armoires as you is vain, darling."

Violet gasped again, but she winked at Kate before facing her betrothed. "Did you hear that? Vain!"

Jack wasn't distracted by her antics as he looked her over, those penetrating eyes taking in her figure, her skin, her eyes. He could probably guess her weight to the ounce. "Eat," Jack said. "Stop going hungry. You don't want your dress to hang off of you. What will that do to your vanity?"

She narrowed her gaze on him, and he held out his hands in surrender. Begrudgingly she dug through her plate again and took a hearty bite of her sausage. "Are you happy now?"

"Maybe if you add some toast and eggs, love."

Violet looked away to find Victor and Kate watching them as though it were a tennis match, their gazes darting between Violet and Jack. The twins stared at each other, in a silent battle, reading the other's mind. Victor had enough worry in his gaze that she begrudgingly took another bite of sausage. His gaze softened and hers narrowed. Had Victor put Jack up to this? No, she thought as Jack watched her with his too-aware gaze.

She picked the crust off her toast and glanced at Jack, who had turned to his coffee, ignoring the paper to watch Violet eat the toast.

"We'll be at the party," he finally added to the conversation at hand. "Ham called me in for some consult or other, but I should be back in time. Shall I make reservations for dinner?"

"The party starts late," Kate sighed. "Don't they know that some of us are creating life?"

"Oh my dear, sacred vessel." Violet laughed, eyeing her sister-in-law, who was glowing again, beautiful like a star. "Sacrifices must be made to meet the curiosity."

Kate snorted as she handed Victor her a cup for a refill. "I think Algie would object to you referring to his beloved as a curiosity."

"Our goal here," Violet announced, "is to discover if she *is* beloved. Is it her? Or her money? Do any of the Americans realize he's an idiot?" Violet gasped and leaned forward. "Could they know he's an idiot and like him anyway?"

"Perhaps," Victor mused as he handed Kate her English breakfast tea, heavy on the cream, "we like him because he's a fool."

Kate's eyes widened, and then her wicked humor kicked in. "Let's make a game of it."

They all turned to Kate, who explained. "Whoever discovers the truth shall receive a prize. Is he marrying her for love or money?"

"What's the prize?" Violet shot back.

"You choose for me, I'll choose for you. Make it good," Kate offered. "Very good."

They both looked at Victor, who grinned. "I'm in."

The three turned to Jack. "I don't care if he's marrying the American for her money."

"Don't you want the prize?" Violet grabbed his arm as though they were discussing a king's ransom instead of a probable bottle of some kind of alcohol.

"I already have it."

Violet shot him a disgusted look, though she was secretly delighted. "Cheeky lad. I'm meeting with my businessman shortly. I shall leave you to your boring...ah...ness."

"Weak, sister," Victor called, as Violet shut the door to the breakfast room and met Beatrice with her hat and a coat. After her meeting, Violet was having lunch with her friend, Rita Russell, at Hotel Saffron before returning home to make sure that Kate napped the afternoon away so she could enjoy the party. Kate was far too inclined to translate some book for the fun of it or spend the day reading about Scottish lavender or some other such nonsense. She needed to indulge in the wonder of a good nap more often.

CHAPTER TWO

*V*iolet's dress for Algie's party took her longer than she'd have liked. The truth was, as she faced her armoire she was weighing the fact that where her cousin, Algernon, showed up, his sometime-friend, sometime-enemy was too likely to appear. Theodophilus Smythe-Hill had been the man who taught Violet very clearly that women were physically weaker than men. Even though she knew that Jack and Victor would leap to her defense, the knowledge left her with a shiver of alarm.

She finally chose a black dress embroidered with black and silver. She wrapped her black pearls around her neck and loaded her wrists with her favorite diamond bangles. Her earbobs were large and eye-catching. There was no scenario where she went to her cousin's party afraid of some random man who dared to place his hands on her once before. She wasn't just going to go, she was going to go and shine.

Violet crimped her hair with the iron, leaving herself with marcel waves. She added dark shadow around her eyes, drew in her eyebrows, rouged and powdered her cheeks, and finished with a brilliant red lipstick. Her makeup, jewelry, and dress were the pinnacle of a Bright Young Thing.

Theo and all of his ilk could learn that women like Violet were not theirs to manhandle. For the sake of sheer common sense, however, she chose low heeled shoes that were easy to move in and a dress that allowed her freedom. If she were going to knee a man in his most delicate area, she was going to do it with all the vigor she possessed.

Violet hurried down the steps and found that everyone else was waiting for her.

"Darling Vi!" Kate breathed, and then twirled her finger, demanding that Violet spin. She did so with a flourish. "Every man at the party will be envious of Jack!"

"They already are," Victor said dryly. "They have been since they've heard the rumors of just how extensive Vi's fortune is."

Violet gasped as Kate elbowed Victor.

"Where is the party?" Jack asked as he held Violet's coat for her.

"Hotel Saffron," Victor replied. "The Americans took the second floor there since some heiress has the whole of the penthouse. Algie said that Mr. Roche was quite upset until he saw the second floor was as lush."

Violet laughed. "I wonder if I saw Algie's heiress earlier. I was there for lunch with Rita. She's the one with the penthouse. She took it for two years, paid it outright, and then went to Yugoslovia. She moved in her books and all her adventuring gear and then fled after what happened with her aunt. She's only just returned."

"She didn't move back in with her father?" Kate let Victor slide her into her fur coat before taking his arm. "I would have thought she would."

Rita Russell's very young stepmother had been murdered, which had uncovered the murder of Rita's own mother. Before they realized it was the aunt who had done the killing, Rita and her father were the suspects.

"Mr. Russell sold the house he'd bought for Melody and moved to a hunting lodge in Scotland. Rita travels up rather often and goes fishing with him. They play rounds of golf and putter about whatever loch he lives by, and then she comes back to London where there are parties, Indian food, and you know...me."

Jack laughed and tangled their fingers together as they went down the front steps to the auto. They were settled and moving again before

Violet realized how quiet Jack was while they motored through the crowded London streets.

"You working inside that head of yours?" Victor asked Jack, seeming to understand exactly his thoughts. Or maybe they were just having the same thoughts. "Catching killers and destroying burglary rings?"

"Just thinking of a case of one of Ham's new detectives. Ham was a bit distracted and disappeared halfway through the consultation with the new fellow."

"Ham is delicious lately," Kate added. "He's almost as bulky as you and in the good way these days."

"Ah, Kate?" Victor said, turning her face to his. "Do I need to worry about this sudden interest in Ham?"

"He is an intriguing hunk of a man," Violet added, just to watch Victor squirm. "Not a tender, ah, slice." She giggled, not able to sustain the ruse, and Kate's giggle had Victor relaxing.

"If you had held back the laugh, my girl, you'd have succeeded with this farce." Kate adjusted her shoulders and wrapped her arm through Victor's. Vi's twin was staring down at his wife with a besotted expression, his vulnerability caught by a nearby lantern.

"What intrigues me," Victor said idly, "is the way that Jack didn't react at all. Are you listening, my lad? Or are you just unbothered at the idea of Violet chasing Ham?"

Jack turned from the window and cleared his throat. "Vi would drive Ham mad in three days."

The auto stopped in front of Hotel Saffron, and one of the staff ran down the stairs and opened the door. Jack stepped out to the sound of Victor's cackles, handing Violet out without the flicker of a perturbed lash.

"Is that Ham?" Violet asked, looking up the sidewalk. "Ham!" He turned and glanced towards them, and Violet gasped dramatically. "Oh my! He is svelte. With that bald head of his, and his new frame, he's like a gentlemen pirate."

"Be concerned," Victor advised Jack.

"He looks good in evening wear," Kate added, waving her face as if she were hot.

Ham nodded towards their group but a shout had them all turning. They saw two shadows struggling in the alley. Ham made a sharp turn into the alley and hauled out a struggling man in a tuxedo a mere breath of a moment later.

"And dragging men around," Violet cooed as Kate sighed. Victor shot a quelling look to Violet. She grinned at her twin. "There's just something very compelling about a beastly kind of man."

The second man appeared and attacked the one in Ham's hands. Victor adjusted his coat, straightened his shoulders, and glanced back at his wife before bravely darting in between the fighting men, leaving Kate giggling while Violet smothered her laughter into Jack's arm.

"You two are evil," Jack told them.

Ham stepped between the two men with Victor at the ready. Whatever Ham said had one of the men hurrying back into the hotel and the other storming off down the street.

Ham and Victor rejoined them, their gazes darting between Vi and Kate who were both trying to smother their laughter. "Is all well?" Ham asked, not even out of breath from the altercation.

"They haven't even started drinking yet," Jack sighed, shaking his friend's hand. "What was all that about?"

"It was Theo," Victor said, "and an American. Ghastly lad. The fellow quite insulted our Ham for stopping the battle even though Theo had left his mark."

"Smythe-Hill?" Jack asked dangerously while Violet carefully tried to hide all reaction.

"How odd," Vi muttered, not thinking about her words. The whole of her friend group turned on her. She held up surrendering hands and said, "Theo crossed my mind this afternoon. That is all." She tried for a cheery grin. "Perhaps I am psychic."

"Mmm." Jack took her hand and pulled her under his arm.

"Let's go in. Risking oneself is thirsty work." Victor stepped in, taking Kate and gathering the attention from Violet. She winked at him when Jack was turned away, and her twin nodded slightly, but Violet reminded herself that she wouldn't let any hard-handed man lessen her.

"Then Ham must need a drink." Her laughter took them up the

steps and into the hotel lobby as Kate pressed her fingers to her lips and Victor scowled at them both.

"You're devils. Both of you."

"Pretty devils," Ham added, innocently holding out his arm for Kate when Victor crossed to the elevator. Kate took his arm, grinning innocently as Victor glanced back, saw them, and glared. "You are looking positively radiant, my dear. Motherhood becomes you."

Kate patted his arm, letting her fingers linger a bit long on his bicep just to torture her husband, and then said a little too loud, "You look too handsome, Ham. Whatever have you been up to?"

He blushed a little and then slid out of grasp, pushing her lightly at Victor as Violet wiped away a tear from laughter. She almost couldn't catch her breath between Jack's silent amusement, Ham's baffled confusion, and Victor's unwarranted jealousy.

"Have I missed something of importance?" Ham asked Jack.

"The girls have recognized you've slimmed down and been doing those exercises. They've been teasing Victor the whole of the ride."

Ham blushed again, glancing away and shuffling a little. Violet grinned delightedly at his bashfulness while Kate announced, "Oh my goodness! Who knew a blush was quite so attractive?"

Violet's head cocked and then she asked seriously, "Are you well, Ham? You were perfect before, don't you know?"

His blush deepened even further. "Just looking for a change, I suppose."

She used her free arm to pull him closer to her. "As long as you know we adore you either way. Are we going to this same party? You visiting the Roche millionaire?"

"I met Mr. Roche when he visited Scotland Yard. He wanted a tour, and it was decided that I would be the guide. I'm afraid I quite abandoned Jack with one of my newer, greener detectives."

Vi's brows lifted at his tone. He sounded both disgruntled and irritated.

"To be honest, I was ordered to be here tonight and be obliging. I feel like a performing bear. I'd have been a little less reluctant if I knew you were coming."

"Our cousin," Vi said, gesturing between herself and Victor, "is marrying the Roche daughter. One of the Roche daughters? Is there just one?"

Vi glanced around and they all shrugged. No one was quite sure of the details of this family. Ham and Jack adjusted to shop talk while Victor whispered to Kate. He was, no doubt, flattering her aggressively.

Vi was unbothered to be left to her own devices. She quite liked the inside of her head when she wasn't blue. The elevator doors opened onto the ballroom floor, and the room was already crowded. There were hundreds of people, and they seemed to be from all walks of life. The intellectual set who was far more inclined to set aside fashion for their own style, artists and dancers Violet recognized mingled with a bankrupt noble who had cosied up to Violet's stepmother.

The smoke was thick above the room, and Violet noted the band playing in the corner; waiters moved among the group with nibbles and drinks, but there was also a bar on the side of the room that had quite a crowd around it.

Violet stepped into the room immediately, leaving her friends behind to see who was there. She guessed that Gerald would be in attendance. Technically, Algie was the twins' cousin on their mother's side, but he was connected enough that Isolde and Tomas would attend.

If their friends John and Gwen Davies were in town, they would be here. Violet saw Rita Russell and Jack's former-fiancé, Emily Allen, taking a drink from one of the waiters. They were with several others Violet recognized from the Piccadilly Ladies Club.

Vi spied her sister dancing with her new husband.

A moment later, someone took hold of Violet's arm, and she spun to see her oldest brother, Gerald, grinning down at her.

"Violet, darling! I was hoping I'd see you and just as I did, you came through the doors as though called to save me from the title-hunters." He leaned in and kissed her cheek and then whispered, "Algie's fiancé has a younger sister who has made it clear she'd like to buy herself a titled husband."

Vi gasped and squeezed his hands. "Well if you do make a purchase,

Lady Eleanor would be happy enough to see you settle some of your fortune on our young wart of a brother, Geoffrey. Perhaps if he's settled, she'll be less grasping. Tell me, Gerald, are you willing to sacrifice for your family?"

"Alas," he said dryly, "I already told all of them I wasn't for sale, when my disinterest wasn't sufficient."

She dragged him back to Victor and Kate and found that Lila and Denny, her dearest friends, had appeared.

Jack took in Gerald and shook his hand. "We're going for drinks," he told Vi, and he and Ham disappeared towards the bar.

Vi spun on her twin and his wife along with Lila and Denny. "What are you waiting for? Play, already! Dance with me, Gerald!" Violet's order left her older brother unfazed, but he obligingly dove into the dance floor with her until Jack collected Violet, handing both her and Gerald a drink.

"Your cousin is this way. His future father-in-law has kidnapped Ham, who needs saving before he destroys his career." Jack's gaze was worried, which shot alarm through Violet. Usually when Jack was upset, one never even knew.

"Shall I step out on you and demand my *very good friend* back?"

"Whatever it takes to save Ham," Jack said. "He has the expression on his face that would have sent me fleeing during the war."

Violet nodded and took the drink before putting on a flirty look and glancing back at Jack. "Time to be inane and a little rude." She sipped the drink. "What a lovely drink. It will fortify me nicely."

"I guess they brought their own barman. Please save Ham."

Vi's brows lifted and she glanced at the bar where a man moved the bottles as though he were a dancer. He made the drinks with a flair that seemed to be choreographed.

Violet hurried to the corner where a loud man held court and wormed her way into the group, weaving her arm through Ham's as she shimmied a little. She tried for an expression to match what she imagined Algie was wearing, sort of good-natured and foolish.

Vi grinned around the group that had taken possession of Ham. With a hidden wince, she noticed that it included Emily Allen, but also Rita Russell. There was a loud, older American man she suspected was Mr. Roche, along with several others she didn't recognize.

"Who's this?" the American demanded with a hearty guffaw.

"Ah," Ham started and his gaze widened on Vi, seemingly alarmed at her appearance.

"Lady Violet Carlyle," she said, holding out her hand to the man. "Ham is my *very* dear friend."

"Things have changed here," the man said, laughing. He had a prodigious mustache, twinkling blue eyes, and the frame and musculature of a much younger man. "Robert Roche, my dear. Or do I say, my lady? I've heard the name Carlyle rather a lot lately. Tale after tale about the Carlyle twins and their pet inspector. That must be you, Barnes. Wouldn't have thought it of you after what your superiors said."

Violet's expression froze at the sound of Miss Allen's amused snort and the description of Jack.

She hid her annoyance with an idiotic laugh. "Where is Algie?"

"Around," Mr. Roche said vaguely. "Really now, what do I call you? It's not *you* who is the earl. Do you go by Lady? Is it honorable? This nonsense is impossible to follow."

"You may call me Violet," Violet said cheerily. "Why stumble over titles?"

"Violet Carlyle," Mr. Roche mused with an interested expression. "I believe you're the one who snagged the inheritance. Algie told me and Clara all about it."

"Earned it," Rita cut in dryly. "I've met all the possible heirs now. Vi was the only one who met Mrs. Davies's requirements."

Mr. Roche lifted a brow, and Violet saw the cleverness that was hidden behind the abrasive man. There was an animal intelligence that had pulled him from nothing to mountains of bullion. She had been raised by a woman with the same calculating gaze.

"Requirements?" Mr. Roche demanded loudly. "What were those?"

"My great aunt wished to leave her money to someone who could manage it without losing it," Violet said with a chipper air that did not match his question. She knew all too well she looked like a bright young idiot.

Mr. Roche glanced Violet over, seeing what she wanted him to. "And she left it to *you?* I wouldn't have thought a young lady like yourself would have much of a head for business."

"I suppose that would be because you're a man and limited by a male's imagination," Violet snapped, losing patience with her game. Rita grinned at the shift, and Miss Allen let out another of those amused, disdainful snorts.

Mr. Roche, however, shouted with laughter. His bright gaze fixed on her and he guffawed again. "I believe you've got me there, my dear. Not fair to assume all women are like my sweet Clara and gentle Malinda."

Rita grinned, gaze lingering on where Violet had taken hold of Ham, before she explained. "Mrs. Davies rather notoriously made her own fortune. I suppose she was inclined to recognize the business acumen of women."

"Quite so," Mr. Roche said, as though he hadn't just made it seem as though such a thing was impossible. "My sweet Clara is a good girl inclined to listen to her papa about everything but marrying this lad of hers. I told her your Algie was a bit of boob."

Violet grinned at that and winked at him, putting back on her silly act as she said, "Well, I wouldn't marry Algie, either. I suppose there's no accounting for a woman's taste or skills."

Ham glanced at Violet and then back at Mr. Roche, shuffling before he lightly tugged on Vi's arm.

"How do you really know this gentleman?" Mr. Roche asked, and Violet had to bite back a demand of what business it was of his. He had rubbed her the wrong way, loud and rude and used to getting his own way. Her sense of humor kicked enough to remind her she was quite used to getting her own way as well.

She grinned merrily. "Ham is my friend."

"But he's a Scotland Yard detective and you're an earl's daughter." Mr. Roche seemed to think that Vi was trying to swindle him, though why anyone would show up at a party and lie about who was their friend was uncertain.

"Our class differences mean less and less as days go by, don't you think?" she shot back, protectively tucking Ham a little closer.

"That nonsense means very little in the US of A," the man said happily and quite loudly, "but I've been given to understand that such things are of greater import here."

"Ham is my friend," Violet repeated.

"Why?"

"He's a dragon behind an affable face."

"He seems rather different," Mr. Roche returned. His eyes were alight with the banter, and she could see that he enjoyed being the powerhouse in the room.

Ham, however, was tense and she didn't blame him, ordered as he was to be there by his superiors and muzzled to protect his job.

"No defense?" He followed it up with a hearty laugh as though he'd won some sort of debate.

"Mr. Roche." Violet exchanged her barely touched cocktail from the waiter who approached the group simply to look frivolous. "You have met and talked with Ham over the course of an afternoon. I've known him for years and seen him work. I just witnessed him separate men fighting on the street and he walked away unruffled. With all due respect," she added, though she wasn't sure he deserved any, "Ham is much more than you realize, and he has been requested elsewhere."

She winked at Rita, shot Miss Allen a nasty glance, and grinned at Mr. Roche before hauling Ham away.

"Jack sent you?" he asked as they made their escape.

"With permission to step out on him if necessary."

Ham laughed with relief. "I was talking to Miss Russell and the next thing I knew Mr. Roche was wishing for me to be a performing monkey for him. It's like he has an entourage as large as the queen's."

"Yes, yes," Violet told him with a wink. "Take a deep breath my good man. I flashed that noble brow and demanded my friend, and now you may rage with Jack and drink too many cocktails. What I want to know is whether his daughter and Algie are marrying for love. Or is there something else happening here?"

Ham sighed. "If that man doesn't like Algie, you won't have to work very hard to discover it. It's difficult to say whether he doesn't thus far. I've seen him insult about everyone around here, and they simply laugh it off."

Violet frowned and then sighed. "I might have to actually sleuth this out. How wearisome."

"Why?"

She grinned as she confessed. "To win against Kate and Victor of course."

"Of course," Ham said as they reached Jack. Ham handed Violet over to Jack and took Jack's whiskey from him. "I owe you for that, my friend."

"I believe I still owe you for my life a time or two. We'll evaluate our debts later."

"You may, however, buy me some chocolate," Violet told Ham. She turned to Jack and grinned up at him. "Dance with me, almost-husband?"

"Always, almost-wife."

CHAPTER THREE

*V*iolet left Jack after several songs, pleading for a cocktail while she headed towards the balcony. Her black dress covered her shoulders and went up to her neck with black lace. although the silk ended at her chest—a choice she regretted now that she was attempting not to melt from exertion and the heat of the packed space by retreating into the night air.

Jack had made his way to Vi's brother, Gerald, where Ham was as well. They were talking, once again, with Mr. Roche, so Violet supposed it was a mission of mercy.

She had little desire to step into that madness again, so she turned away and watched through the windows of the French doors for her cousin, Algie. Vi had *every* desire to meet his betrothed but every time she glimpsed him, he was surrounded.

Algernon Allyn was an affable cousin, and she loved him rather like she'd love anyone who was related to her and she'd been raised with. They had little in common beyond being sent to stay with the same great aunt over the holidays. Violet had spent more Christmases with Algie than she had with her younger sister. She'd lit more yule logs, hung more stockings, decorated more trees with Algie than anyone except her twin. Then there were the afternoons fishing, swimming, and adventuring on their childish journeys in the woods. She, Victor, Algie, and—on occasion—a few other cousins. All that being said, when he wasn't around, she didn't miss him.

Violet moved across the wide balcony to the rail and took in a deep breath of the cool evening air, letting it out slowly. She had cooled down quickly to nearly cold and decided to go step back into the ballroom until Jack returned with her and would give her his arm or his jacket. She knew Jack would escape to the balcony in a moment with Ham, and they'd have a cigarette and discuss whatever case was bothering the two of them.

She turned for the doors and found Theodophilus Smythe-Hill blocking the way.

"Didn't I see you get thrown out of the hotel already?" she asked with an arched brow. "Tell me, did you have to bribe your way in or did you terrorize some maid at the servant's entrance?"

His face flushed but he spoke mockingly. "If it isn't the frigid *Lady* Violet. Tell me, have you bought your husband yet or is it still possible for him to escape?"

"If I were looking to buy a husband," Violet shot back, "I'd have gone with the bargain version—you."

His gaze narrowed on her and then he glanced over his shoulder. No one had noticed them. He pushed her back onto the balcony, shutting the French door behind him. "All alone, Lady Violet? Where's your uppity maid?"

He took hold of her arm, fingers digging in, making her gasp in pain, and without even thinking, she twisted away, using the move she'd practiced for months in her jiu jitsu lessons. She hooked one leg behind his, shoved just so, and punched him on the way down. The second he hit the ground, she kicked him in the kidneys, then backed away out of reach.

"I don't need my maid or my Jack to deal with the likes of you," she said. She walked to the French doors as though her heart wasn't racing, and her hands weren't shaking.

As she reached for the door, Jack opened it. He took in the fingerprints on her arm that she was just starting to really feel, the wild look in her gaze, and the way her chest was heaving. He placed both hands on her waist, lifted her and turned, handing her like a child to Ham. She'd have objected if that familiar gaze of Jack's weren't so cold and terrifying. A moment later, Jack shut the balcony door behind him.

"What was all that?" Ham asked with a gaze that was totally unlike Jack's while also having the same all-seeing, penetrating nature.

"Theo."

Ham cursed and then looked about. He waved at someone, Vi didn't see who, but she was handed off once again, this time to Rita Russell and Gerald, and Ham followed Jack through the doors and onto the balcony.

"Hullo there, luv," Gerald said, entirely missing what was happening.

"Where did Mr. Barnes go?" Rita asked without the same lack of vision. "Is everything all right?"

The sound of a fist smacking flesh carried through the slight opening of French doors.

"Oh I say," Gerald said. "Who is that? Sounds like a boxing match."

"It's Jack," Rita said, shooting Gerald a baffled look. "Is he really your brother?" she asked Vi. "He's very different from you."

"Well now." Gerald sniffed. "We can't all be first class in the brainwork."

There was another sound of a fist hitting flesh and Vi flinched. She glanced around, looking for Victor and found him with Kate and their best friends, Denny and Lila. She shot Victor a look and he lifted his brows. Her expression become only more intense until her twin gathered up their friends and joined them.

As they arrived, the sound of Theo cursing hit all of them at once.

"I say," Gerald said once again in distress.

"I say," Denny said with a delighted air that was followed by the sound of another fist and Denny's giggle.

"I say," Victor said with a gaze narrowed on the forming bruises on Violet's arm. "I say," he said again, letting go of Kate's arm and opening the French door.

"Get back," Ham shouted as Jack threw Theo through the doors. Theo hit the ballroom floor and slid across the shining floor, his pomaded hair flopping about like a broken wing.

Jack stepped through the door, entirely unruffled. He picked up Theo by the lapels and walked him across the ballroom floor and through the crowd. Vi's gaze fixated on her fiancé, and she told the others idly, "I took care of it."

"Not apparently to a sufficient extent," Lila said with a bored air and then kissed Rita's cheek as though they were meeting on a Parisian street rather than after a body had just parted through their group. "Rita darling!"

"I say!" Denny muttered. "There was no need to end things just as I arrived. Jack has little regard for my wants."

Victor followed after Jack with a growl, Ham alongside him. They rushed at the end as they saw Jack shove Theo through the doors to the stairs.

"Do you think he'd throw him all the way down the stairs?" Lila asked with that same bored air.

"Your brother just shifted from a...a...a...lapdog to a wolf before my eyes." Rita glanced around them, shocked. "Is it always like this with you?"

"Lion," Violet and Kate both said and then grinned at each other. Violet finished, "That's who he really is. The rest is an act."

"No," Denny moaned, "decidedly not. The excitement is between all the boredom. Hunting murderers between nonsense like cocktails and Cuba."

"Cuba?" Rita sounded intrigued as Mr. Roche approached the group.

"Didn't seem to be your affable dragon dragging out that young blighter, Theo." Mr. Roche's bright, happy eyes had faded. "Come with me," he ordered.

The group of friends glanced at each other and then back at Mr. Roche, making no signs of moving.

"Please," he said more generously, almost pleading. "Please."

"Vi, is everything all right?" Vi's sister, Isolde, stood behind Mr. Roche with Tomas on her arm, and Violet nodded distractedly. She glanced about, noting the sharp gaze of Miss Allen and the onlookers with lifted eyebrows and whispers behind their hands. They had drawn quite a crowd.

"Please, Lady Violet, please. I need your help. You and your affable dragon."

"Jack?" Rita asked as they followed Mr. Roche from the ballroom and up the stairs to his suite. Isolde and Gerald remained behind with Tomas to try to allay rumors, but Violet didn't think there would be any avoiding the talk.

Vi shook her head to answer Rita but didn't speak as they situated themselves in a lushly appointed sitting room. A servant was sent out for cocktails and Mr. Barnes. Mr. Roche had apparently not made the connection that Violet's man was Jack. Or perhaps, the American wanted Ham's help and intended to get Violet to manipulate him?

"Where shall I look for him, sir?" the butler asked as Vi narrowed her gaze on the two, trying to figure out Roche's game.

"Try finding the big one with bloody knuckles," Denny told the servant. "That's your man. Bring both of the men with them." He faced Violet. "Why does he think you're with Mr. Barnes?"

"She told me so," Mr. Roche said, scowling at Rita. "Why are you here?"

"You gathered all of us," Rita told him. "I was standing right there."

"Where is Algie?" Vi added, ignoring the others. Maybe he could translate what was happening here.

"They're coming." Mr. Roche settled himself in a chair near the fireplace rather like a man who was settling into a throne. "I need your help. You and your Ham."

"Your Ham?" Rita asked, echoed by Denny and Lila.

Violet sighed. "Jack is mine. Ham is our friend."

"You told me that he was your *very dear friend.*"

"I meant it," Violet replied. "He's just not my future husband. Mr. Roche, Jack and I are not going to help you with whatever this is. We're getting married on Saturday morning and then we're leaving."

Mr. Roche blinked. "I thought you were with that investigator. Miss Allen told me that very specifically."

"Jack is an investigator, but we're not going to be distracted from our upcoming wedding to help with whatever this is."

Algie and a little blonde entered the room. She was the size of a pixie and wearing a vibrant magenta dress. Her long strand of pearls was interspersed with diamonds, and she also wore a thick diamond choker. Violet had overloaded on diamonds and jewelry that evening and she didn't even come close to what the blonde was wearing.

"Vi!" Algie called affably. "Victor! Everyone meet Clara, my beloved." Oh, dim Algie. He hadn't even realized that Victor wasn't in the room.

Violet's and Kate's gazes met, and they both considered the assertion that Clara was beloved before unitedly shaking their heads. More proof was needed before Violet or Kate would believe such a thing and win the bet. Especially from Algie, who told a slew of lies in his day.

"I'm so glad you were able to come." Algie cleared his throat and grinned at everyone before he frowned. "Where *is* Victor? I just assumed he was here. Where is Jack? I was telling Father Roche all about your clever gent."

"I thought it was Mr. Barnes." Mr. Roche sniffed and then muttered, "You led me to believe that it was that Yard man."

"Barnes?" Algie laughed. "Well by Jove! I never did say his name, did I? The clever Yard man. I can see why you'd jump to...well, no I can't, I mean, that chubby man? For Vi? *Lady* Vi? Maybe if she were homely, but Vi's all right."

"Oh Algie," the pixie Clara laughed, "stow it before you make life-long enemies. I'm Clara, so nice to meet all of you. Papa, did you ask?"

"She says no. We'll ask her man."

Algie snorted, and Denny out and out laughed as he took a cocktail from the returning servant.

"What's this now? She wear the pants?"

"Vi—" Algie whined. "We need you. Please? Please, Vi?"

"No," Violet said, flatly.

"What if we just tell you about it?"

"You could throw a body into my lap," Violet told him, "and I wouldn't help you find the killer let alone whatever you need help with. I'm getting *married* on Saturday. Whatever you have an issue with is not my problem, not right now."

"Quite right," Kate agreed, nodding firmly as the door to the suite opened and Jack, Ham, and Victor entered the rooms smelling of cigar smoke.

"Now which one of these fellows is your man?" Mr. Roche demanded as he stood and stepped forward.

"They all are hers," Lila told him. "Victor Carlyle, her twin." Victor bowed. "Ham, her friend and blood-brother type friend of her beloved." Hamilton nodded. "And Jack Wakefield, her affianced."

"You all missed an intriguing offer while you were smoking cigars and getting a bit of air," Violet said with a narrowed gaze on them.

Jack held out his hand and lifted his brows in silent question.

"Robert Roche," Mr. Roche said, shaking hands. "My daughter is determined to marry your—what did you call Barnes?" Mr. Roche glanced at Violet and then back to the others. "An affable dragon? Algie is the affable buffoon."

Denny laughed, rubbing his hands together in glee as Mr. Roche continued. "Seems to me that your Jack is the dragon here."

"But not affable," Jack told him, crossing to Violet and taking a seat on the arm of her chair. "What's all this?"

"They want our help." Violet didn't expand.

"We're getting married within the week and leaving the country for an extended period," Jack said flatly. "No. Perhaps you can manipulate the Yard into forcing Ham to help you."

"I have a job," Ham said with a political smile. "I can assure you that my time is taken. If you need an investigator, I would admit to knowing a few private ones who are quite clever. Unless, of course, you wish to make an official complaint?"

"Stanley?" Jack suggested, his hand settling on Vi's arm just above where Theo had left his mark. "Shall we go? I find my patience for humanity is quite expired."

"No, no, we need your help," Mr. Roche said loudly. "Surely you can just listen."

"Theo was at your party," Victor told Algie with the same expression that had once threatened to remove Algie from their lives if he continued to associate with the man.

"Not by our invite," Clara piped in while Rita barely bit back a question. She was too new of a friend to know that Theo had once tried for Violet's hand rather forcefully.

Violet sighed and stretched her neck. Why had they let themselves get pulled into this?

Algie's Clara almost growled as she added, "That man is an out-and-out rat! He's weaseled his way into my brother's and cousin's lives."

"Put a hand to your pockets," Victor told Roche, already knowing the end of the story and glancing overtly at Algie, who had once been in debt to Theo and escaped only by Violet's mercy.

"I know," Algie declared. "I told them! Everything, I swear."

Violet searched Algie's face. "Everything?" she demanded.

"Everything," he solemnly swore.

"It's love," Violet shouted, just beating out Victor and Kate.

"Damn it!" Victor muttered. "If it's not a good prize, love, she'll never let us hear the end of it."

"What's all this?" Mr. Roche demanded. "What prize?"

"You don't want to know," Jack told him. "So your boys got involved with Theo. That's hardly our problem. Even if we sometimes claim Algie."

"It's worse than you know," Mr. Roche told them. "My Bartholomew is all set to marry his love. It *is* love. She's a good girl, good family, good fortune. She's all you could want, and her father won't put up with a bit of nonsense. Somehow this *Theodophilus* has some information about Barty before he straightened out his life. Wild oats. Nothing that couldn't be—"

Violet lifted a brow and then added for him, "Covered up?"

Mr. Roche sniffed. "The details aren't important if we can't count on you."

"You can't," Violet told him. "We are getting married and that is it."

CHAPTER FOUR

"*L*et's have a party." Violet shifted in the auto, stretching her back, as they made their way home, and snuggled closer into Jack's arms. "Something ridiculous."

The unacknowledged tension in the auto with what had happened with Theo and Jack's reaction was making it seem as though they were terrible actors for a play that no one had rehearsed for.

"You put him on the ground yourself," Kate said with a wooden merriness. "Jiu jitsu lessons have been worth it."

"I did." Vi sighed and glanced out the window. She wasn't afraid, but she was disturbed that it had happened at all. Did men treat each other this way? Or was it just how they treated women? Like someone you could simply overpower or manipulate. Whoever was the biggest or the strongest got their way?

"Good job," Victor cheered quietly and Kate elbowed him.

Vi's mouth twisted. "It's not surprising that Algie harped on about us to the future in-laws. He loves a good story, and ours are exciting from the outside. What's shocking really is that someone like Robert Roche thought he could just tell you help him."

"He did offer money," Kate said as though that somehow made it better.

"We can't be purchased like a...a...race horse!" Victor scowled.

"They didn't want *you*," Violet laughed. She lifted Jack's hand from his lap and placed it on her own. She rubbed her thumb over his knuckles where they were bruised. The middle one had cracked.

"It's like I said," Jack said, low, "we're notorious. I want one of your cocktails, Victor, and perhaps a cigar. This party was a failure, and I am battling a rage headache. The way that man treated Ham like a servant. As though Ham weren't better than the both of us."

"That does sound lovely," Violet lied. She wanted to curl up in Jack's arms, but Denny had announced as they left that they were coming over to cleanse their palettes. She wasn't sure what they were cleansing, but Violet didn't really care. She hoped that Denny was bright enough to bring sweets. "But we were discussing a party. Something spur of the moment, I think. Roller skates in the ballroom, perhaps. A scavenger hunt through the rooms we haven't fully explored. Shall we christen our house, Jack?"

He pressed his chin onto the top of her head, lifting up long enough to drop a kiss on her head, then settled her back into his arm.

The auto arrived, and just ahead of them were Isolde and Tomas. "We were hoping you'd come back here," Isolde called from the behind the gate. "Tomas wants a cocktail."

"And a cigar," Jack said as he opened the gate for Violet.

"I would take one of those," Denny said as he joined them with Lila on his arm. "I've got chocolate for Vi. I assumed you already had ginger wine since she'll be questioning the nature of mankind and will need to relive all the terrible things that have ever happened. Lila says we should leave her be, but I think we should get it out in the open."

Vi scowled at Denny as Rita approached from a black cab.

"I think we've already got our party," Kate said, holding out a hand to Rita to welcome her in. "Cocktail, darling?"

"May I?" Rita glanced about. "I wasn't sure that I would be crashing, but well—"

Violet gasped as Jack lifted her and carried her through the gate, running up the steps. "Everyone in," he called. "No one else is welcome. Quick, shut the door before Algie appears with his tiny female."

"Really now?" They all turned and found Ham walking down the street. "And what about me?"

"Get in here, old man," Jack called as Hargreaves opened the door. "The door is getting locked and we're not at home."

Jack shifted Violet so she was hanging over his shoulder and moved inside to the shouts of laughter. Slowly, he slid her down his body while everyone else greeted each other outside. "We aren't going to turn our minds to the nature of mankind," Jack told her, putting his finger under her chin. He slowly tilted her face towards his and placed a kiss on her forehead and another on each temple. "We are going to turn our minds to our honeymoon and the life we're crafting after that. Nothing else. Not Theo, not how mankind treats each other, not all the bad things in this life. Just the good."

She grinned at him. Denny whistled behind them. When they spun, Denny shrugged. "You left the door open and told us to come inside."

Rita placed a hand over her chest. "That was perfection. The most romantic thing I have ever seen."

"It was pretty romantic," Isolde added, wiping away a tear.

"By Jove!" Violet said to Jack, but her gaze remained fixed on her younger sister. Blonde, lush, lovely, and a little green about the gills now that Violet focused on her. "They're all mad, and Isolde is weeping over us."

"She's got to be expecting," Jack finished, certainly noting all the things that Vi had seen. Their gazes met before turning on Isolde and Tomas. "Someone's in trouble with her daddy," Jack said with a smirk.

"Not a good place to be," Denny told Tomas, who was both somehow pale and blushing. He was grey with circles of red on his cheeks and the tips of his ears.

"The *earl* is going to slaughter you slowly," Victor told Tomas, who swallowed thickly.

Kate squealed, and Jack and Violet grinned at each other while Kate threw herself at Isolde, begging for a confirmation of the truth.

"We won that round, I think," Jack told Vi, who nuzzled his chest before stepping away. She reached her younger sister and kissed Isolde on the cheek.

Hargreaves had opened the parlor door, and a maid had already appeared and left, following Hargreaves's low order. Denny grabbed Victor and nudged him towards the bar while they all settled into their favorite seats. Violet noted how Ham's gaze lingered on Rita, but she seemed unaware. She was lovely, Violet thought, but more so, she was adventurous, clever, and fun while Ham was dedicated to his career.

"So, a party then?" Kate asked as she and Isolde snuggled into the same seat to whisper together over their shared experience.

"Tuesday night?" Denny begged. "We're supposed to go to some official dinner, and we hardly can if our dearest friends are having an— an—"

"At home," Lila finished as Denny started handing around drinks. "Now someone explain to me why this American fellow thought you'd work for him in the days before your wedding. I wasn't paying attention when he was speaking."

"Lila," Denny told her, "you are the queen of my heart."

"Mine too." Violet lifted a hand to her ears and pulled off her earbobs, letting them fall to the table next to her, sliding her bangles off as well. "Did you agree to work for him, Ham?"

He shot her an irritated glance. "Didn't have much of a choice, really. He ended up pulling in my superior who made it clear that I was to set aside my actual work—but not really—and do this as well. This Roche fellow is the kind of rich that makes everyone sit up and take notice."

Rita laughed at that, and Violet smirked as she told Rita, "You are too, my dear. Or your father is."

"As are you," Rita shot back, taking a cocktail from Victor and smiling happily down at it. "Those G&Ts at the party were so heavy on the gin, I might have grown another eyeball or something equally terrible."

"I like them heavy on the gin," Denny told them, propping up his feet and crossing his legs. "We should have a baby too, Lila. Isolde and Tomas are passing us by."

She just shot him a look. "What did you see, Rita? After we left? Anything? Or before we got there?"

Violet scowled at Lila. "I know what you're doing, Lila Lancaster."

Lila grinned evilly, not admitting that she was trying to draw Jack and Violet into the case. Lila lifted her brows to emphasize her question to Rita.

She answered slowly. "I...there has been a lot of fighting. I even complained to the management."

Violet glanced at Jack, who reached out and covered her ears. "We're not getting involved."

Violet took one hand and pulled it down to her lap. "We could just advise Ham. Our roles have been reversed. He'll interfere and do things that he wouldn't normally. Perhaps use the at-the-ready Rita to pry into things, given she's staying in the same hotel."

"I could do that," Rita said, looking interested.

Violet hid a grin behind her hand as she saw Ham struggle with his instincts. He both wanted Rita working with him to spend more time with her and wanted to keep her away because she was calling to the man in him. Ham, like Jack, was a man who'd prefer a woman to be safe and secure.

Before Ham could say no, Rita continued. "The Bartholomew Mr. Roche was talking about just arrived in London after having traveled with his fiancé to Paris. That's where your cousin met them."

"Look at Rita knowing more than you and I about Algie," Victor said. "It's the woman's ear for gossip."

"As if you don't gossip," Kate said, rising from her whispered conversation with Isolde to tease her husband. "You'd have all the details if you were staying in the same hotel as Algie. Especially given how loud Mr. Roche is."

"Tell us about the fiancé," Lila said. "This good girl with money. Have you met her?"

"I have," Rita admitted. "Her name is Bettie Keys. She's quite lovely, quite sweet, and quite rich. The Bartholomew *isn't* the son, it's the nephew. So he needs money a bit more."

Violet laughed and then told Victor, "It's Algie's question. Is it love of the woman or love of the money? Can she really be all that wonderful? Sweet, beautiful, and rich? Surely, one of those is a lie."

"It isn't with you," Jack told Violet.

Victor and Denny immediately said, "Violet's not sweet."

"What about Rita?" Lila asked musingly. "She's lovely, obviously. And rich."

"She helped trap her aunt," Rita answered. "She refuses to follow expectations and will travel the world despite her father's objections to things like African safaris. She's not sweet either."

"She's also talking about herself in the third person," Victor said, wincing.

Rita grinned wickedly. "She knew that she was too new to the group for anyone to be comfortable telling the truth about her."

"But she wants to stay?" Lila asked.

"She does," Rita said, glancing around. "Shall I beg? Or offer to do some sort of entrance hijinks?"

"How do you feel about roller-skating?" Violet asked, as though she were seriously going to give Rita an entrance project.

"I feel good about that," Rita said. "I'm not sure I ever have."

"She's a willing roller-skater, she likes cocktails, she shops, she gossips for clues," Violet answered. "Turns out we were missing someone and never knew."

CHAPTER FIVE

Their first party was starting in hours, and Violet and Jack had escaped to the local park with her—their—dog. The little red-brown spaniel was running through the park, spinning circles, chasing leaves, and then dodging back to circle her slower walkers. They trailed after the exuberant Rouge with their arms twined together.

"It feels a little odd," Violet told him, looking up at him through her lashes, "to be having a party and it being at our home. I felt as if I were an imposter when I talked to the servants about the evening."

Jack laughed, squeezing her fingers and turning when the wind kicked up, blocking her from the sudden swirl. "I wonder if people always feel like imposters. Sometimes when I go to a new town on a case, I find myself wondering why anyone would turn to me and take my opinion. They don't know me from anyone else."

"Perhaps some people are endlessly struggling with the idea that they're in a position that shouldn't be there. I can, however, assure you," Violet laughed, "that Lady Eleanor does not feel like an imposter."

"Or maybe she does," Jack shot back with a devil's twinkle in his gaze. "Maybe she is endlessly comparing herself to your father's other wives."

"And feeling like the one who doesn't belong? I don't know. I think my mother would have been far more the one who felt as if she'd stepped onto the wrong stage. According to Aunt Agatha, Mama was like Rita Russell. Adventurous and bored by *society*. Perhaps Father was endlessly baffled by her. Perhaps if she hadn't gotten sick, she'd have disappeared like Rita does. I think Lady Eleanor is just like the nobles' wives."

"What about Gerald's mother?"

Violet shrugged. She had no idea about her father's first wife. She was the mother of Violet's three oldest brothers, but only Gerald yet survived. "Will you marry again, if I die?" Violet asked, and Jack scowled at her.

"You aren't going to die." It was an out and out order with a bit of a growl at the end. "Getting over Emily was one thing. Actually losing *you?* No."

"I'd marry again," Violet said, but Jack knew her well enough to catch the smirk in her voice.

He spun her around, holding her at her waist and pressed against her body. The look he gave her was so—fervent—she had to fan herself. "You won't be getting the chance either."

"There's the new divorce act," Violet suggested.

"That only works if either of us have lovers. I won't be stepping out on you, my love. And any lovers of yours wouldn't survive the night to admit to cuckolding me, let alone confessing to a jury of any...activities."

"Oh ho." Violet stepped back with a dramatic gasp. "Murder, I say! Murder and from a Yard man!"

"I've gone back into semi-retirement," Jack told her. "Practically speaking, I'm just a man."

"Can such things be?"

He snorted and took her hand again, wrapping it around his elbow. "Of course not. I am a man among men."

"A pearl of great price!" She laughed, grabbing her side. "Suddenly it's funny again! My favorite joke given life again. A second, better life! I can't wait to use it until it's dead again."

Jack grunted, but Vi heard the humor in the noise.

"Listen," Jack told her. "I might be a pearl of great price—"

Before he could finish, Violet was laughing again, too hard to hear him. Once she stopped, she said, "Oh, you are! What lucky woman was clever enough to trap you?"

"A clever minx. Bright-eyed. Vivacious. A little too much devil in her."

Violet laughed again. "Now tell me…is this woman—this devil of yours—attractive because she's wealthy? I've heard you trapped yourself a rich devil at least."

"What cares one for such fripperies?" Jack asked, running his finger down her arm. That heated look was back in his gaze, and she wasn't quite sure how to handle it in the middle of the park, so she called for Rouge instead. "Are we going back?"

"I suppose we must since we've sent Beatrice for every pair of roller skates she can find, ordered masses of small mouthfuls to be carried about on trays, and raided Victor's cellar."

"Did we raid it?"

"He was rather willing," Violet admitted. "Possibly because I would have enjoyed taking it anyway given how we took all of that chocolate liqueur."

Jack laughed again, tucking her closer to him as they cross the street and headed into Victor's house. Violet's maid and the other servants had moved most of her things over. She felt a little bit like a traveler to her own house with the final trunk ready to take the last of her things. Her luggage was packed for the honeymoon; however, they still needed to gather up her typewriter, her paper and pens, and makeup.

Certainly Beatrice had a rather extensive list of things to gather for Violet, so she could be as spoiled as always and have whatever she wished. Violet took a long breath in. "Upon a moment of personal reflection, I have been forced to realize that my life is rather wonderful."

"Is it?" Jack's mouth twitched at the corners, but he didn't laugh at her.

"You really are a pearl of great price." She patted his cheek. "So I think you should be the imposter to make sure things are ready for the party." She laughed and ran inside, leaving him at the front door, and skipped up the steps to her bedroom.

There were several dresses she'd bought for the parties and teas around her wedding day, but she still had one or two Jack hadn't seen yet. She wanted to bring back that heated look to his eyes, so she took the most unique of her dresses. It was a nude sheath dress that hugged her from her chest to her knees with enough of an A-line to allow for dancing. Overlaying it all was a black lace dress, embroidered with flowers that reached to her mid-calves, allowing, she hoped, for a short enough dress to roller skate in.

She layered around her neck the turquoise beaded necklace that was as long as her longest strands of pearls. Next, she placed the diamond collar that Jack had bought her for Christmas on her neck. On her wrists were the diamond and turquoise bangles that had been made for her as well. On her fingers, she wore only her engagement ring. She wanted it to stand out like a lantern on a hill. She was affianced and soon to be wed. Nothing gave her greater happiness at that moment.

Violet held her short hair back from her face with a turquoise, black bead, and black feather headpiece. She added makeup rather heavily, ending it all with a wine red lipstick. With her full dress in place, Violet glanced down at Rouge, who gazed up at her with pleading eyes.

"Did you want to go, darling?"

Rouge's tail slammed against the door frantically as though she could provide a yes using her tail thumps as Morse code.

"You'll have to get gussied up."

Rouge seemed to understand well enough to bark twice.

"All right then." Violet dug through her jewelry until she found a ribbon to tie around the dog's neck. She added to the bow a diamond and ruby broach that belonged to Aunt Agatha and then kissed the top of the dog's head, leaving behind a trace of lipstick.

Violet touched up her lipstick and then crossed to Victor and Kate's bedroom door and knocked.

"Come in!" Kate called. "Come see the spectacle. A beached whale in pearls."

Violet pushed the door open dramatically and gasped, "Where?"

"Here!" Kate moaned.

"For the love of all that is holy, Violet," Victor begged. "Tell her she is beautiful."

"Kate!" Violet moaned, "You are lovely! My goodness woman! Have you seen your skin? You glow! Have you seen your eyes?"

"Look at my feet," Kate wailed, and Violet glanced down and gasped, which made Kate actually burst into tears.

"Violet," Victor groaned.

"What happened?" Vi gasped, reaching down to touch Kate's foot with a solitary finger. "Is it contagious?"

"Yes!" Kate shouted. "Jack will eventually give it to you and then you'll have pig's haunches for feet to stumble about on."

"I don't think you can skate on those," Violet told her. "I wasn't sure it was a good idea before I saw those ham haunches, given my Violet Junior you're growing."

Kate was still crying. Violet cocked her head and examined her sister-in-law. "My goodness woman, stem those tears."

"But it's your first party, and I want to go." She ended on a wail, and Violet pressed her hand against Kate's mouth to muffle the crying. Kate's eyes widened in a fury that Violet had never seen from her sister-in-law before.

"You're in trouble now," Victor declared. "I tried that once, and she threw a shoe at me."

Violet's expression turned evil, and Victor shook his head frantically, but Violet couldn't help herself. "It's a good thing, then," Violet laughed, "that she can't fit a shoe on those feet."

Kate gasped behind Violet's hand and lunged, but the baby mound was too much and Kate fell back into her seat. "I'll get you," she shouted and then added on a moan, "when I can run again. I will chase you down and tear out your hair."

"Victor," Violet laughed from the doorway. "You married a vixen!"

She hurried into her bedroom, ringing the bell for Beatrice.

"Quick darling," Violet ordered, "we need those slippers. The ones that just cover the toes and tie with ribbons."

Beatrice nodded.

"I'm afraid Kate's feet have become rather swollen, and she's weeping about it. Hurry now."

Beatrice darted from the room to where Violet's already packed trunks were stored. It took her a good quarter of an hour, but she returned nearly breathless with the shoes.

"I think I shall also have to go crawling."

Beatrice's gaze widened, but Violet didn't explain. She crossed to Victor's door and opened it without knocking, since she didn't expect them to let her in without persuasion. She found Victor kneeling in front of Kate, dabbing her eyes, and Violet sighed.

"You are my favorite couple."

Kate's gaze narrowed on Violet, who held up the slippers.

"I come bearing gifts. They'd look lovely, I think, with your silver and white dress. Though not as lovely as your face or your soul."

"Bah!" Kate said.

"The loveliest soul I have ever seen."

Kate's lips twitched.

"Beautiful really. Like a sunset over the ocean. Like the moon with the merest wisps of clouds only emphasizing the light of the moon."

"Stop it," Kate demanded.

"Like a pearl in a perfect setting."

"You are terrible at this," Victor told her. "I'm ashamed of you. As my twin, the greater twin, fools might say, I'd think you'd be better."

"Fools?" Violet snorted. "I suppose that might be accurate. You know I never saw you as the lesser twin. How could I when you somehow captured the heart of this splendid creature?"

"Much better," Kate said, seeming to feel a little better. "I did like that one."

"I'm clever," Violet agreed. "Not as clever as Kate, of course, but clever enough."

"Now that was good, appealing to her vanity." Victor winced when Kate shot him a nasty glance.

"Darling Kate, sister of my heart," Violet said, "favorite of my people. Swollen from growing a magical creature. Please, sweet one, please tie on these shoes and come to my party. I won't have it without you, darling. Shall I cancel it? Put up a sign on the door? We'll curl up here in your bedroom and eat chocolate and send Victor for trifle after trifle until he's sweating and flustered."

"Perhaps..." Kate mused.

"Doesn't that sound fun? A good alternative if my ribbons aren't long enough." Violet's sardonic voice sent her into giggles, and she ran from the room before Kate could throw the slipper. Violet shut the door behind her and heard the echo of the slipper hitting the wood.

CHAPTER SIX

heir ballroom was ridiculous, Violet thought, as she spun in the center, taking in the display. The dark hardwood floors had been shined to the extent that the lights reflected in the wood. The chandeliers were half-lit and flickering. They probably should have had them wired with electric light, but Violet adored candlelight.

A jazz band was setting up in the balcony that looked down onto the ballroom. Once upon a time a string quartet or something to that effect would have played there while debutantes spun in pale dresses on the floor below. For that evening, the band would wail songs while their friends roller-skated and indulged in cocktails, chocolates, and other small bites.

It would be merry and fun, and add the flavor Violet wanted for her home. Frivolous and friendly with dashes of intellect. Violet smirked at her thoughts as she heard someone behind her.

"It's hard to believe we used to share that two-room flat, isn't it?" Victor asked. "How things have changed."

Vi looked at her twin over her shoulder and lifted her brows in a silent question.

"Kate decided to lie on the chaise lounge in your boudoir until everyone arrives. She's got her feet propped up as though gravity will suction all that fluid out of her ankles."

Violet's lips twitched, and she bit her bottom lip to stop her laugh.

"It's terrible," Victor told her righteously, but she could see the devil in his gaze.

"Terrible," Violet agreed. "Just awful."

He coughed to hide his laugh, and a giggle escaped Violet.

"Do you miss the flat days?" Violet asked, suddenly serious.

Victor's gaze flit over hers. "You're not getting cold feet, are you? I'm not entirely sure Jack would let you go if you decided to scamper."

Violet shook her head. "It's this place. It makes me think about the other places that felt like home. Only our rooms at Aunt Agatha's, that horrid flat, and your house."

"This house will feel like home," Victor told her. "I'm not sure mine will feel right with you even a few doors down."

Violet's eyes burned at that admission. It was her largest worry too. "Shall we have sleepovers? There's a likely bedroom in the other wing for you and Kate."

"Maybe we should just dig a tunnel from my house to yours."

"Why wouldn't we?"

Victor laughed. "We are heirs now. Rich, bright young things. What else would we do but dig a tunnel?"

"Well," Violet mused, "we could buy the houses between us, tear them down, and have a massive shared garden."

"Or rent them out but make a passage between our houses."

"Maybe we could just sublet the back of their gardens for our secret alley."

"Or build a bridge? Some arch over the two gardens to ease our transit."

"Or," Jack said from the doorway, "you could—and I'm just throwing out ideas here—use the sidewalk."

"But then people would know we were sneaking to visit each other at 3:00 a.m."

"They already know that. Midnight story plans, random pranks, fighting just to see the other one blow their top. Everyone who knows

you knows that neither of you have any boundaries. Not even when
normal people sleep."

Violet and Victor hooked their arms together and asked in unison,
"So?"

Victor glanced at Vi, smirked, and added, "He's holding grudges
because I woke you up the other day to help me figure out the problem
with the detective story."

Jack laughed. "Just commenting on facts."

"Are those Christmas light strands?" Victor asked to change the
subject, since facts inevitably won fights.

"They are." Violet reached up to the French doors that were
framed in Christmas lights. "Are they frivolous? Or too much?"

"Appropriately frivolous for a roller-skating in the ballroom party
with jazz and cocktails. The tables with the vases are, perhaps, too
staid for this party."

Violet ignored him. She liked the dichotomy between the traditional decor and the light strands. "Don't forget the chocolate, and the
odd little mouthfuls that the cook is making us to go along with
shrimp pots and mushroom toast."

The doorbell rang. Victor checked his watch. "Oh look," he said,
"now you're the hosts. Are you up for it, pretty devil?"

"I'm just going to pretend I am," she told her twin, grinning at his
matching face. His own grin echoed hers.

"That's what I've been doing." Victor shook hands with Jack as he
added, "Congratulations on the house, old top. The house, the party,
the wife-to-be. I can assure you that you'll never be bored."

"I've noticed that bit," Jack said. "Are you handing her over then?"

Victor shook his head. "She'll always be mine. I'll always be hers. I
guess I'll just take you too."

"What's all this?" a voice from the ballroom door asked. "Serious-
ness? Who loves who best? You all love me best," their friend Denny
declared from the doorway. He smoothed back his hair and adjusted
his coat. He'd been trimming down since Ham started, as if admitting
he didn't want to be the chubbiest of the group. It only spurred Ham
on. "Head's up, lads. There were others behind us."

Lila, his wife, glanced his way and lifted both of her brows. "Laddie, even I don't love you best. Vi, my favorite, it's only Isolde and Tomas. No need to worry yet."

Denny clutched his heart and then told Victor, "Get to the cocktails, old man. I need a good one."

"We've hired a barman," Jack told Denny. "So Victor can play with Vi and girl Friday for his wife."

"Don't be daft, man. The barman is for the plebeians. I want a Victor cocktail."

"Oh it looks lovely!" Isolde said, entering the ballroom. "I think my mother would turn over in her grave, were she dead, if she knew you weren't standing at the door to greet your friends."

"Oh ho!" Victor crowed. "Now Violet will be at a loss of where to greet them. Darling, will you go downstairs? Stand in the doorway of the ballroom? Abandon the greetings, strap on roller skates, and thoughtlessly enjoy yourself?"

Violet shot Victor a useless quelling look and then asked Jack, "Shall we stand here as they come into the ballroom?"

"I have no idea," Jack told her. "Tell me where you want me."

They awkwardly took up position near the doors of the ballroom with Isolde, who seemed to be the only one who had any idea how to handle greeting friends as they entered. It wasn't their first party, but in their own home, it seemed to warrant something more official.

Isolde and Tomas were followed by their eldest brother, Gerald. Ham and Rita came in at the same time, seemingly by accident. Rita was laughing at something Ham said before she leaned in and kissed the air next to Violet's cheek to prevent a brick red smudge.

"Look," Rita said, "we're lipstick twins."

"I'm so excited to join in on the frivolities, Vi!" Isolde said, spinning. "What fun this is."

Victor handed the earliest arrivals cocktails before allowing the barman to take over. Violet accepted her bee's knees in one of the new cocktail glasses she'd bought just weeks ago. The pretty glass seemed to make the sweet, honeyed taste of her drink particularly delightful.

A whole slew of more casual friends arrived, interspersed by her cousin with his American family, including the father, who shot both Violet and Jack an angry look before taking a cocktail and refusing roller skates. It wasn't until the party was in full swing that Violet finally met Bartholomew and his fiancé, Gertrude. The girl, with a low bun, a pursed mouth, and stiff shoulders, shook her head at both the offered cocktail and the roller skates, and her love only hid his irritation at her circumspect choices when she couldn't see him.

"True love," Lila muttered to Violet and Rita. They'd all caught the interaction between the couple before Barty took her away for some air in the gardens.

"I'm not saying I want to live the teetotaler life." Rita tucked a stray hair back into her headpiece and adjusted her scarlet red dress. "But I will say that if you don't want to live it either, then don't marry a woman who does."

"He's not marrying her for her values," Lila said, without trying to adjust her tone. "He's after her for her money. It's as clear on the nose on her face."

"Mmmm," Rita agreed.

"I don't care," Violet lied, then considered. "No, I actually don't care. Not right now. It's time for roller skates and refills, loves. Only Kate gets a pass at playing with me on the dance floor...skating floor? Whatever is the official term?"

"If it isn't love," Lila said, ignoring Vi's question, "do you think she knows? Why does she want him? Is she in love and hoping she can change him? I always despise when women think they can change some poor lad to make them what they want. Marry the man in front of you."

"I'm not sure I want to marry," Rita said as she put on her skates. It was a thoughtless aside before she added, "Now, before you scold me, I think you should know that despite having seen lions in their natural habitat, having ridden elephants on multiple occasions, and once having had a monkey as a pet, I have never roller-skated."

"Uh oh," Lila said. "You need help."

"You know who's very good? Shockingly so?" Violet glanced around the room for Ham, met his gaze easily since he was looking their way, and then waved him over. "Hamilton Barnes."

Violet handed Rita into Ham's willing hands and then turned to Lila, who slowly lifted an eyebrow.

"And just," Lila said, "after hearing her say she didn't want to marry. Lady Violet, you interfering minx! If ever a man was made for marriage and family, it's that one. He's already half in love with Kate's baby and has stars in his eyes when he looks at Rita."

"I just want my friends to be friends," Violet lied with a wink. She stood up carefully on her own skates. "I'm two cocktails in. Shall I break my ankle before the wedding, do you think? How elegant shall I be on crutches and a train to my dress?"

Lila lifted a brow at someone behind Vi, and she felt the press of a large warm body against hers. Almost a living wall. She grinned up at him, still facing the other way.

"What do you think? Shall I break myself and we'll have to call things off?"

"You can't escape me that easily," Jack told her as Violet lost her balance and her feet started to shoot out from her. He caught her easily.

"I'd hobble down the aisle, darling. No need to worry on that front." As she spoke, Jack lifted her, turning her and providing a steady arm.

Jack wasn't wearing skates but his grip let Violet spin out with an arm to the ceiling. Her dress twirled around her legs and she spun back to him, noting that Lila stepped away to Denny, who wore skates and spun her onto the floor.

"Shall we learn how to tango on our honeymoon?" she asked Jack.

"If you want." He grinned at her. For once, he wasn't hiding his expressions. Usually only she, maybe Victor, and almost certainly Ham saw what Jack truly felt. Tonight, however, there was a lightness in his gaze, an overt happiness that set her heart afloat. "Whatever you want."

"I want to tango. Then I want to tango in Spain. We'll be put to shame by those who were born with the tango in their blood, but it will be fun anyway."

"All right," he said, sending her spinning and catching her before she fell. "I suppose we can do that. Shall we run with the bulls?"

As he caught her against his chest after a particularly wild spin, she asked him, "Are we going to Spain on our honeymoon? Is that why you're so willing?"

He grinned at her and shrugged without an answer.

Her gaze narrowed on his, but—if anything—his amusement became more apparent, his grin wider, the smirk in his gaze all the brighter. Violet placed both hands against his chest, glanced behind her, and pushed off. She had caught the rhythm of the skates and was almost dancing on wheels as the next song started.

Jack let her escape him as she joined the dancing skaters. The trumpeter was simply fabulous. The music wailed over the ballroom, and when Violet paused against the wall, catching her breath, she could see that her friends were having fun.

There was laughter in the air, thickened with smoke from cigarettes and candles. The crowd around the bar wasn't so thick that people were waiting a long time, but someone had assigned another servant, and Violet would see that the servant was working as a girl Friday to the barman, keeping things running smoothly while the expertise was working.

Violet caught sight of the ballroom's chaise lounge. There was a small table next to the lounge, but both of them had been abandoned, and she spied Victor dancing with Kate. They were more to the side of ballroom away from some of the wilder roller skaters, but Victor suddenly stopped, pulling Kate into his body.

Violet expected to see her brother kiss his wife senseless, but instead, he turned, tucking Kate behind in that protective move Violet knew so well. The spaniel front that Victor normally wore faded, and Violet felt a flash of alarm. Her gaze darted about the room, looking for the threat, and stopped in horror when she saw Jack.

Jack held a struggling Theo by one arm.

She could hear his rage. He was shouting so loud that people had back away, forming a circle. Violet dropped to her knee and pulled off her skates as quickly as she could.

"We all know you're marrying her for the money. Stupid woman that she is, she doesn't even know it. Do you want to tell her? Tell her how you were engaged once before? Tell her how you loved Emily

Allen? That you might as well have been living together with all that entails."

Violet could feel the gazes on her. She wanted to close her eyes and take in what had just been said, but there were too many gazes on her, with even the band clanging to a stop. With focus, she breathed easily, but each careful movement was painful. She wouldn't let this snake ruin her. No one needed to know that she was withering inside.

Violet both knew the frantic, wild-eyed fury of Theo's expression and the cold, rigid rage of Jack's. His gaze landed on hers, and she knew that the statement was true. He had been sleeping with Miss Allen before she'd thrown him over. And not how he slept with Vi.

Violet wanted to call to Victor to help Jack to get Theo and his poison away. Theo's ringing, hate-filled laugh reached her like the pounding of fists, and she broke her nail on her skate. She pulled it off and slowly rose to her feet.

The entire room was facing her, and Theo laughed hysterically.

"Look at her. Did I break your heart, *Lady* Violet? You think you're so good. So clever. So smart. You're just another stupid—" The word he used was cut off by Jack's hand over his mouth, but she knew what Theo had said, and it had been foul.

"Victor!" Violet called to her brother, who had shaken off his shock and made his way to her. "Help Jack remove the trash."

Theo reached out and grabbed a vase from one of the pedestal tables, slinging it wildly at Jack, but Jack ducked as Theo let go, and it crashed onto the floor. The few who hadn't noticed the fisticuffs noticed it then.

Before Victor could reach him, Jack had already hauled Theo to the French doors. Theo fought wildly, grabbing onto the doorframe of the door and catching only the cord of the electric light strand. He yanked it free, sending the glass bulbs into a spray of sharp pieces across the wooden floors.

One of the weaker women shrieked while Lila's lazy muse cut through the shock with a, "Well that will be expensive. It's a good thing Vi and Jack are so rich. Someone send for a broom. What nonsense and vile hatred."

Violet appreciated Lila's quick lies on Jack's behalf. Vi nodded at a servant, "Clean it up, please."

"You there," Isolde called. "Turn up the lights. You, start that band back up. Nothing to worry about, everyone." She called merrily. "Just a jealous drunk who needs some fresh air."

It took several measures for the band to catch their rhythm. Violet stared in shock after Jack. They were supposed to christen their house with frivolity, fun, and friendship. Not...not that!

She wasn't thinking about the other part of it. When people had stopped staring at her, she let herself close her eyes and take in a deep breath before putting back on her own happy mask. Spaniel? Fluff-headed fool? Whatever mask she wore, she hoped it sold her unconcern.

Victor glanced Vi over. "Stiff upper lip, darling. These things happen with cocktails."

Vi took a deep breath in. There was something ineffably painful in having someone who knew her well enough to read the depths of her, who loved her, and felt her hurt *with* her.

"How did he know you were having a party?" Rita demanded, fury shrouding her movements and tone. "None of you would have invited him."

"A very good question," Victor said, placing a steadying hand on Violet's lower back. His fingers dug in enough to help anchor her.

"Hmm," Ham mused, his too sharp gaze on Violet. "Shall we go after them?"

"He has a cigar in his coat," Victor answered. "I'm sure Jack will smoke it and walk off his temper."

"Of course he will," Ham agreed. "I'm always game for one those Cuban cigars of his."

Both of them looked to Violet, who repeated Rita's question from before. "How did Theo know we were having a party?"

"I told him," Robert Roche answered without a shade of regret. "If you won't help me willingly, perhaps you'll help yourselves in getting rid of him." Behind Robert Roche stood Vi's cousin Algie and his fiancé, Clara.

CHAPTER SEVEN

"Oh no, Father Roche!" Algie said, shooting Violet a pleading look that begged her to see him as innocent.

"Daddy!" Clara scolded. Her gaze was curious and fixed on Violet.

"We need the best. Algie says these two are the best. This nonsense of Theo trying to blackmail our family needs to stop before it causes real damage."

"Mr. Barnes," Rita snapped, "is on the case. He's an excellent investigator."

"He's not who Algie said was the best."

"He is, however, Jack's boss and friend," Rita said, shocked. She sounded as if she couldn't believe that Mr. Roche was such a dullard.

Violet breathed more deeply, grateful that the attention had turned from her to Roche. She needed a moment. Just a little moment. It wasn't as if she'd expected that Jack had never...she knew that wasn't the case. It was just...it was just...oh!

"I don't know how you do things in America," Violet told Roche coolly, forcing herself to focus on him rather than on her racing thoughts. "Thrusting yourself into our lives and demanding your way and our help will not be a successful tactic."

"It's not the American way," Clara said, still giving her father furious looks. "It's Father's way! Papa, this is my new family. How could you?" She crossed her arms and stomped a foot, looking like a child throwing a fit. "They'll never accept me now, and Algie simply idolizes them!"

"You aren't the only duckling in my nest, duckie," Mr. Roche told her flatly. "You know that—" He trailed off at the sight of Gertrude, Barty's fiancé, and lamely finished, "I care about all of my children."

"Then," Lila told him too loudly, "you would put all of them in your will and remove certain issues." She cared very little that she'd turned the attention to Barty. "Look at that. One simple change," Lila added, "and the problem is solved. We can all go back to our lives without Theo *or* you."

Violet shook her head and crossed to the bar, demanding a drink while servants swept up the broken glass. She needed to get away from Victor's ability to telepathically read her, and from Roche before she murdered him in front of the crowd. "Ginger wine."

The barman glanced at her. "I'm afraid I don't have that."

"It's the bottle with the stars at the back of the bar," Violet told him. "Pour me a rather generous glass."

He lifted his brows but didn't argue. Violet hadn't been the one who hired him, and she hadn't interacted with him yet, so he had no idea that this was her house or that her maid had ensured that her favorite ginger wine was available in every bar in the house. It didn't matter.

A few people had gamely started skating again, and as Violet walked back to her party with her ginger wine, she reflected that she might not have christened her house with the right kind of party, but at least she wasn't bored.

Rouge bounded out from under Kate's chaise lounge where Victor's wife was sitting as Violet approached.

"Are you all right?"

"Sure," Vi lied. "How are you feeling? How are your poor feet?"

"Not too fast, Violet. Are you all right?"

"Sure," Vi lied again, pasting on a failure of a smile.

"You know that Jack isn't as innocent as you are, don't you? He's quite a bit older than us."

"No woman wants a face to go with the names, Kate. My frivolous christening of my home was ruined by a rude American and—once again—that snake Theo. But I'm fine."

Kate scoffed.

"I'll be fine," Violet told her. "Let's leave it be, shall we?"

"Of course," Kate said, with a weighty gaze that promised she'd wind back around to Violet's feelings and prod them until certain Vi was in good shape.

"Where did the Americans go?" Violet asked, glancing towards where Denny, Lila, Isolde, Tomas, and Victor were watching Vi carefully. Algie was speaking quickly to Victor, but Vi could tell that Victor wasn't listening. Clara, Algie's fiancé, was standing next to her beloved, nodding. "She really does love him, doesn't she?"

"Yes, she does love him. It's clear she's besotted with Algie for some odd reason. The rest of her family, though? They scattered when you just spun on your heel and stalked off. The elder Roche said they'd let you get your womanly ways in hand and wait for the hysterics to settle."

Vi's gaze narrowed, and she stared at Kate, who was fighting a grin. Instead of giving that the response it deserved, Violet sipped her ginger wine. Rouge leapt up onto the chaise lounge where the two of them sat side-by-side. Vi was far too aware of the sympathetic and smirking glances that were sent her way.

They weren't really talking, but Violet kept a cherry grin on her face to keep her emotions to herself.

Lila appeared with the bottle of ginger wine while Denny leaned against the wall, holding out a plate of small bites of sweets. Vi took one of the petit fours that belonged at an afternoon tea more than a roller-skating party. When one was entirely out of the norm with a party, Vi had decided that offered bites could be as frivolous as the roller skates.

"Has anyone seen Jack yet?" Denny asked. "Maybe we should go look for him."

Vi wanted nothing more than to look for him, but she had too many alert gazes on her. There would be even more whispers if she went to hunt him down. Now was the time for lingering sips of wine, pretending to laugh, and watching for the Roches. She didn't intend to help them, but she wouldn't mind scuppering their plans. Perhaps she could find Gertrude on her own and explain that her 'righteous' fiancé was a gold-digging, amoral blackguard.

"I'm sure he's fine," Violet said. "Ham would be out there if he thought Jack needed someone. If anyone has ever seen Jack truly upset, it would be Ham." She glanced over and saw Ham standing with Rita. Both of them were watching Vi, and when she met their gazes, theirs jerked away. Ah, Vi thought, even Ham and Rita were talking about her.

She sighed and stood, reaching down to scratch Rouge's ears, noting that her ribbon and broach had turned a little. Vi corrected it and tucked her dog under her arm. Maybe she'd just go ask Victor or Ham to check on Jack. It had been a good half of an hour. Wasn't that enough time to cool off, smoke your cigar, and come back to put on a happy face for their guests?

Vi felt certain that it was. Tucking Rouge a little more firmly, she crossed to Victor. He was standing with Algie still, and they were talking quietly.

"What's going on?"

Victor avoided her gaze.

"Sleuthing, brother?"

"You aren't the only witty one."

"The only one," Violet shot back, "who has ever felt that was true was she whose name I won't repeat while so many people are watching my every move."

"Oh," Algie muttered. "I really didn't think he'd be quite so—"

"Careful now." Victor slapped Algie's shoulder. "That's the future in-law. They control more of your happiness than you know. Better to not make any enemies."

"I say," Algie muttered again, shooting Vi a blushing, apologetic look. "I say, Vi, I—"

She shook her head and tucked a loose hair back into her head-piece. "We know you too well for that, Algie darling. Your Clara is simply lovely."

Algie beamed under her compliment. She glanced around, hoping that Jack had returned. He wasn't there and neither were any of Algie's people. Where were they? Had they left? Or were they snooping through her house? Given the number of servants in the ballroom and entrance, she doubted anyone would notice of someone were wandering the halls they hadn't been invited into.

"Why isn't the nephew in the will?" Vi asked, voicing the question that had been bothering her since Lila pointed out the obvious issue.

"Yes, well—" Algie said, blushing.

"They aren't about, old man," Victor assured him. "I've kept a ready eye so I wouldn't have to remove Violet from trying to claw their eyes out."

"Barty's a bit the prodigal son," Algie admitted. "Roche built his fortune, it's true. Only so did his brother. The brother died early and left Barty an heir as soon as he turned eighteen years old."

"Ohhh," Vi said, "bit of a prodigal son?"

Algie winced and nodded. "Lost it all on wine, women, and gambling. The only reason it isn't wide news is that he did it all in Havana. Even married a girl there who died in childbirth. I don't think even Gertrude realizes that the baby is half-Cuban. She just assumes that he fell in with some British girl or something. Romanticized it and all."

Vi's gaze narrowed on her cousin, who flushed.

"Not that it isn't a romantic tragedy," he tried again, and Vi nodded.

"I suppose that Father Roche didn't love the little Cuban daughter-in-law?"

"Indeed, very much no. Isn't too happy about the child either. But more, he says he won't give any money to someone who lost as much as Barty had. Barty made his choices. He can have a job at the company and work to make his fortune again, or he can live the life he created for himself with his eat, drink, and be merry ways."

Rouge whimpered a little, and Violet glanced down at the pup in her arms. "Rouge, darling?"

She whined again, and Violet set the dog down. Perhaps she had her eye on some random morsel someone had dropped on the ballroom floor? Algie grinned at the dog while Victor stepped to the side as Rouge darted at the door.

"Someone needs the ladies," Victor told Vi, and she nodded, following the spaniel to let her into the garden. The gate would allow Rouge to exit the garden, so Violet never let the dog out on her own. When Vi reached the French doors, she saw they'd been closed as Jack took Theo outside. The strand that had been on the doorway was gone, and the long string of windows were all lit except one.

Rouge pranced at the door, whimpering, and Vi frowned at her. The little dog was usually better behaved. Perhaps she really had received some bite that was too rich for the little beast. Vi opened the door, and Rouge darted out into the darkness.

Instead of her usual quiet move to do her business, Rouge barked frantically as she ran down the steps and around the house. Vi's gaze widened, and she glanced over her shoulder, waving Victor after her. Something was certainly wrong. Rouge was far too well-behaved for such nonsense.

Vi rushed after the dog, knowing Victor would be hurrying after her. She wasn't afraid, but she was concerned. Perhaps there was a rat in the gardens? Perhaps some young rogue who'd decided to peek into the windows and see what the party was all about?

"Rouge?" Jack's deep voice asked. "How did you get out here?"

"Oh Jack!" Violet said, feeling suddenly awkward.

He gasped. "I suppose I shouldn't be surprised you'd appear just now."

She stepped back, hand to her chest. What was that supposed to mean? She wasn't hunting him down to box his ears, only letting her dog...she gasped.

"Yes," he said to her unvoiced question. "Yes, it's a body."

"Who is it?"

"Theo."

Violet stepped back farther.

"I didn't do it," he told her, sounding as offended as she'd been a mere breath ago.

"I know! Just, Theo. By Jove, Jack, it's—"

"What's all this?" Victor asked. "All well, Vi?" The protective note in his tone was a clear warning for Jack.

"No," Violet said, feeling the horror of it. Her gaze was fixated on the body. Rouge growled under Jack's arm. At his feet was the dead shadowed heap of the man she'd hated the most. The man she loved the most stood over him, and this...this...well—all was *not* well. Not well at all.

CHAPTER EIGHT

*V*iolet pressed her hand over her mouth, making no attempt to hide her distress. Jack had sent Victor for Ham, and at the view of the body, Ham shed his affable friend persona. He was just *all* dragon. All of that fire, that penetrating gaze, that...that...*everything* —and it was focused on Jack.

Vi watched Ham carefully. He was asking questions, and Jack answered just as precisely. They seemed almost like puppets enacting a play without conveying any of the necessary emotion.

"Bloody hell," Violet ground out, digging her fingernails into her palm.

Ham was over there blithely asking questions and taking notes. Notes! The fiend! As though Jack were a suspect. Vi bit down on her bottom lip. Of course Jack was a suspect. What had they told Roche? Someone could throw a body in their laps, and they wouldn't help. Why, by Jove, why had they tempted fate like that? She felt as though some mischievous sprite had taken note and decided to force them to action.

Violet had never bothered to watch the official investigative process personally. She had never cared before now, and to see it as two best friends—brothers really—force themselves to enact this mockery.

She was about to box both of their ears. This was no time for proce-
dure. Vi would break every rule there was to free Jack. Her gaze landed
on him, but she avoided his eyes. She was too close to the edge; seeing
anything at all in his gaze would send her into the abyss. Seeing it first-
hand was something she very much didn't want to see on the night of
her party.

"It'll all work out, Vi," Victor lied. She didn't bother to mock him.
They were both all too well aware that Jack would be a suspect *and* that
her wedding was days away. He knew she didn't believe him, she knew
he didn't believe himself. She didn't even answer him, just glanced his
way, saw Kate approaching gingerly with Rita and jerked her head at
Victor, so he'd see too.

He rushed to Kate's side while Violet firmly grasped the reins of
her emotions. Kate joined Violet, Victor, and Rita a moment later,
gaze solidly fixed on Violet. "It'll be all right, Vi," Kate lied. The careful, tender voice was enough to send Violet right over the edge, so she
dug her nails into her palms. She didn't need sympathy or love or any
sort of emotion except anger. Anything more, and she'd fall apart.

"Of course it will be fine." Rita's fury made Violet feel a little
better, and Vi dared to meet the very blue gaze. "We'll make it so.
There's a series of hurdles ahead. That's all. You can do this. You and
Jack aren't alone in this fight, Vi."

Hurdles, Violet thought and nodded at Rita. Hurdles, yes. Nothing
more than a few obstacles and then a honeymoon. Vi would think of
them exactly like that. She glanced at Jack, saw his too-knowing gaze
take in all she was trying to hide and immediately jerked her own eyes
away.

Did Violet think that Jack would go to jail for killing Theo? No.
No, she didn't. She couldn't let that happen. The first hurdle would be
to get them past that threat.

Except...did Violet expect her stepmother in the morning? Yes.
Reporters, certainly. Her stomach churned. She could only imagine
what Lady Eleanor would do. The delay of her wedding? Very probably.
Just because Vi knew that Jack hadn't done more than rough up
Theodophilus Smythe-Hill didn't mean that Jack wasn't the *main*
suspect.

Anything else would make this death and the subsequent investigation look like a conspiracy to cover up the murder. Jack had multiple
altercations with Theo, all of which had witnesses. Theo had just upset
Violet the week before Jack and Vi were going to be married and with
intent of ruining things for her, for them. If you assumed Jack were
marrying Violet for her money—he wasn't, but from the outside—well,
Theo had just nearly cost Jack the woman he said he loved and a
mountain of ready money.

Violet closed her eyes against the sight of Victor's worried gaze,
Kate's too-understanding gaze, Rita's overt concern, Ham's careful
questions, and of course—the body. She didn't dare even look at Jack
after that last glimpse. She might collapse like one of her weak hero-
ines, full of tears and wailing at the heavens.

Better to think of the dead man. She'd been so proud to knock him
to the ground at Algie's party. Someone had done a much better job of
it than she had. The image of him—on the ground and cursing at her—
had been replaced with his body. Head turned to the side, staring into
the hedge, eyes not moving, with a knife sticking out of his back, fancy
evening clothes and the night hiding the blood she knew was there.

Violet heard Jack say, "I walked him fully to the gate, Ham. I
watched Theo walk away. How or why he came back, I don't know.
Why was he even here in the first place?"

Ham answered. "Roche invited him to try to compel you to help
him with his blackmail problem."

"That's a better motive for murder than Jack's," Rita told Ham.
"Irritation at the party. Why would Jack kill Theo given all of the
people who truly hate him?"

"Oh, I hate him," Jack said.

Violet shot him a look that told him to shut his mouth, but he
didn't react to her silent order.

"We all know Theo was a snake," Ham told Rita, ignoring Jack. "If
Theo has been blackmailing one person, he could be blackmailing any
of the guests. The entire party is suspect. Some devil saw the altera-
tion between Jack and Theo and decided to rid himself of an expensive
problem, knowing Jack would be the primary suspect."

"Certainly," Victor said, grabbing onto the idea. "There's that bloke that was fighting with Theo in the alleyway before Algie's party, all of Algie's in-laws—except maybe the dames. You invited Lyle Longfellow, didn't you Vi? He's hated Theo since we were ten years old."

Vi nodded.

"Poor Lyle has been under Theo's thumb for ages. Maybe he finally snapped."

"So we're agreed that Jack didn't kill Theo," Vi said, speaking only to Ham.

He nodded, probably trying to convey something assuring in his look, but she didn't *feel* assured. She felt as though she could drown at any second. This wasn't just any murder. It was Jack on the line. Jack's freedom. Jack's future. *Her* future with Jack. The dreams for this house, for eventual children, for books to write and places to visit, and the life they were going to live.

"Ham," she said, her voice breaking before she tried for a cheery grin and failed miserably. "If it's possible..." Vi trailed off at the threat of tears. "God," she muttered, and it was a prayer not a curse. She'd have dropped to her knees in that second and begged without shame if she thought it would save her Jack.

"If it is possible," Ham swore, taking her hand and squeezing it hard, "I will have him, at the altar, on your wedding day. I will do every single thing in my power and the power of Scotland Yard to find the real killer and clear Jack of any suspicion."

She nodded, grabbing hold of those rogue emotions of hers with an iron fist. She glanced at Jack, winced at the look in his gaze, and darted her eyes away from all that he felt combined with what she felt, and it was too much for her to bear with a stiff upper lip.

"We're all hands on deck for this one," Ham told the others. "Everyone we can pull in. Isolde, Tomas, your father"—that bit was directed to Vi and then he glanced at Jack—"and yours. Everyone we can muster is going to help us beat the pavement, the jazz clubs, the offices, whatever it takes. I'll be damned if I see my best friend arrested."

Violet nodded. Melodramatic and a little bit of a prima donna to leave Jack in the garden though it was, she went inside. She walked up the steps past the new butler, ignoring his concerned look. He had to be wondering just what was happening. All they'd done was send a footman for the local police with a note from Ham.

Would Ham work this case himself? She immediately knew he wouldn't. Ham oversaw cases, didn't work them. He'd assign someone ethical, and then Ham would do whatever could be done.

The local police boys had already arrived and made themselves at home. Of course, Vi's sister Isolde had stepped in, controlling the flow of guests, police, and refreshments. She was an excellent hostess, raised to reign as she was at that very moment. Vi stood back from the goings on and watched, trying to keep her mind blank.

Ham returned to the ballroom and gave the police boys instructions about what to ask and to chart the location of who had been where during the party. No explanations were given beyond an unfortunate accident having occurred. Vi heard him tell them to expect an Adam Clarkson.

Maybe Violet should have taken the knife. She could have hidden it where they'd never find it. Professionals or not, Violet knew she'd have succeeded. Of course, Jack would never have let her. She was going to be fighting his honor the whole of this case, she thought.

She glanced at her friends, seeing the Piccadilly Ladies Club members gathering with their dates. They were brought to the policemen working out of Vi's parlor. Vi had a surreal moment where she realized she hadn't sat in that parlor yet and talked with anyone. The police had christened the room for her with their interviews.

Focus, Vi told herself. Focus on the issues at hand. She knew her mind was spinning because she'd tucked away too many emotions and moments of the evening. She needed to curl up in her bed and write them all out into her journal, allowing herself the freedom of confessing all of her emotions and thoughts, be they good or bad, generous or unkind, furious or forgiving.

One of the women of the Piccadilly Ladies Club met Vi's gaze, and Vi found herself looking at Miss Emily Allen, reporter for the Piccadilly Press and one-time betrothed of Jack. Apparently also Jack's one-time lover. Vi refused to linger on that. She'd have guessed if she had bothered to let her thoughts bend that way.

Miss Allen nodded once at Vi. There was no apology in her gaze, and it took Vi a moment to realize that there shouldn't be. What happened before Vi wasn't Vi's concern, and Vi had little doubt that nothing had happened since Violet and Jack had realized they were in love.

Vi's mind scattered again, and she stared up at the ceiling as she remembered the feeling in Bruges. Tomas had followed Vi to ask her— once again—to marry him. Vi had told him she couldn't. She loved another. That was when she hadn't known how Jack felt, and she'd been worried that the attraction between them had died. She'd thought she'd return to London and discover his attention and potential love had turned to another.

The memory of that panic somehow grounded her in the moment. Many things had happened since then, but she knew that Jack was both capable of devoted love and that he adored her with all the love he had to give.

"What's happening, Vi?"

Vi was jerked from her thoughts and found Tomas in front of her. He had never loved her. Seeing him made her smile. "Do you remember all of those proposals?"

He blushed deeply. "I didn't know what love really felt like then."

Vi nodded. "Jack told me that once." She didn't expand as she felt Tomas's worried gaze on her. "Is my brother still here?"

"I thought Victor was with you," Tomas said, looking even more worried.

"Gerald," Vi said. Really, though, it should have been obvious.

"Ah, yes. He was questioned by the police. He, Isolde, and I were the first. Afterwards, he went into the library to steal one of Jack's cigars."

Vi ran her fingers over her lips. "Would you get him to keep Lady Eleanor away tomorrow?"

"Will she be coming?" Tomas demanded.

"Unless you want to tell her about that baby of yours, we're going to get her full attention. The good news is we'll get Father's regardless of the baby. You might just survive Father's anger if you play your cards right."

"What do I do?" Tomas sounded almost desperate.

"I have no idea," Vi confessed. In a low voice she explained what had happened. "The question," Vi finished, "is whether Father wants to rid the family of Jack, regardless of his innocence, or if he's on our side."

"What if Jack isn't cleared, but they can't convict him. Will you stay with him?"

Vi jerked, surprised. "Would you leave Isolde after something like this?"

"If she were the suspect?"

Vi nodded.

"Never."

Vi lifted a brow and then said, "There's your answer."

CHAPTER NINE

*V*iolet ran up the stairs to her boudoir, but she left it carrying an empty journal and a pen, making her way to the balcony area that overlooked the ballroom. She glanced down on the throng. The full lights had been turned on along with the candles in the chandeliers. The floor no longer shone with the dancing and skating. It needed to be polished again.

The banquet tables holding trays of food had been picked over, the sweets were entirely gone, and the barman had stopped making drinks, turning away all requests with an unapologetic shrug. Vi frowned for a moment and then realized the policemen probably had requested the drinks to stop. Better to question people who weren't still working on getting thoroughly zozzled.

Most hadn't realized that someone had died, but they knew something was wrong given the low whispers and the way they were clustered together. People were brought from the ballroom, and they didn't return. Vi did her best to write down as many names as she could. Her lists was pages long, but she needed to be able to rule out who she could.

She'd get Ham to give her the list his men made and compare the two to her guest list. There had been people she'd seen who she hadn't invited. Companions of guests or folks like Theo who had just determined to come. It wasn't as though Violet had sent out official invitations or had servants turning anyone away. They'd answered the door and let in anyone who'd come for the party on the theory that no one would show who wasn't invited. Clearly she could have been more careful, but she hadn't minded sharing cocktails and nibbles with a few uninvited guests as long as they were there to have fun with the rest of them.

Vi breathed in slowly, letting her breath out with a soft hooting. Her mind wasn't thinking so much as stumbling about in thoughtless, useless circles. She bit down hard on her lip and told herself to focus, but she wasn't able to do much more than think of Jack, shudder, and write down another name.

She just *couldn't*. If she thought too hard, all she could see was herself at the aisle waiting for Jack to have him not appear.

She heard a sound behind her and didn't look. It was, of course, Victor since it couldn't be Jack. She wasn't even surprised Victor had found her. He knew her so well, he probably had talked to Tomas, watched the policemen for a few minutes, and then thought: What would Violet do next?

Go get her journal as though it were a security blanket and clutch it, trying to find some resolution. She wasn't surprised when he placed a hand on her back as if to pull her back to herself, but she wasn't ready to face him or what had happened.

"Do you think they'll arrest him?"

"No," Victor told Violet, and she was too panicked to tell if he was lying to her. She looked up at him, begging him to make her believe, and he added, "Ham knows Jack didn't kill Theo. If there is any reason to make a case that Jack didn't do it, Ham will. He promised you so."

"He assigned someone else the case, didn't he?"

Victor's jaw flexed before he nodded once.

"He'd assign someone super ethical. Someone who was good and known for being honest no matter what. Someone who would arrest Jack if he had to."

Victor took in a deep breath. "But we know Jack is innocent."

"*We* do." Violet didn't even try to hide her doubt that anyone else would.

"Which means there is no evidence that Jack killed Theo."

"This was a crime of opportunity," Violet told Victor, having it click together in her mind in a moment. "What do you want to bet that knife is Jack's? Maybe from his office? Maybe from the silver? Who knows where they got it. It wasn't like anything deadly had been hidden away in case a random person decided to use a letter opener"Vi's voice cracked. Their aunt had been murdered with her own letter opener—"or some other likely object. Jack's in trouble, Victor. Comforting lies won't make it any less true."

Victor cleared his throat and glanced below at the ballroom. "There's Lyle Longfellow. He went to school with us. Me, Tomas, Algie, Theo. Poor Lyle's father is a vicar and a believing one too. Not just one of those fellows who fell into the work and says the right things. Lyle has been under Theo's thumb time and again because of the vicar father and Lyle's endless crimes against morality."

Violet nodded.

"The vicar is pretty wealthy too, and he has a son who's a curate or some other such thing. Working his way through the church ranks. Guess who has been threatened to live a righteous life or lose his inheritance?"

"Lyle," Violet said, feeling a flash of rage. "Is he so bad?"

"He's like us, Vi. Lyle likes to dance and sing. He makes a mean old-fashioned and smokes too much. It's not like he has a slew of bastards or committed drunken crimes."

The rage just intensified in sort of a pre-reaction to Lady Eleanor's coming visit. "I am *so tired* of parents thinking they can control us with their money. You know what would be honorable? Not raising your child to expect money and then using it as a—a—whip to make that child do whatever you want even after they are adults."

Victor rubbed Vi's back as though the comfort of her twin would somehow fix things. It wouldn't. It couldn't. Nothing could.

"It's their fault," Vi whispered, letting the first tear fall. "Their fault to expect the unfair. If you want to disinherit a child for thieving or for gambling their allowance away, I can understand. If you want to do it because they love someone honorable but not who you wanted—that's not right. They should have, at the least, made it clear that those choices weren't theirs to make if they wanted money."

"It's not fair to think you can control someone with money. Maybe they should stand on their own, though."

Vi didn't disagree. She was just so angry. If she had to guess at that moment, it would be that someone had murdered Theo to keep their lifestyle. Was it a wild guess into the dark? Yes. She knew it was. Maybe they were hiding a real problem like Barty Roche frittering away his fortune or something that didn't deserve to be hidden, like a legitimate child with a Cuban woman.

Violet curled her hands into fists and turned into Victor's chest, hugging him tightly.

"I'm not thinking clearly," she confessed, pressing her face into him. "What if I lose him?"

"You won't."

Vi looked up at her twin, meeting a gaze that matched what she saw in the mirror every morning. "You can't make that promise."

"If I have to bribe guards and smuggle him to a yacht, you won't lose him."

Violet laughed a wet, woeful sound and then let her forehead fall against his chest. "You know Jack wouldn't let himself be smuggled. He'd just march back to the prison and hand himself over."

"What he'd do to stay with you might surprise you, Vi. We're not going to let it come to that."

"Do you promise?"

"I don't have to promise," Victor said, dropping a kiss on her forehead. "You are brilliant and clever and willing to break the rules and throw a fortune at this problem. I won't need to fix it for you. Darling devil, you know you'll fix things for yourself."

Vi's wet laugh didn't have the same confidence, but it was a good reminder.

"Start by hiring whoever Ham recommends," Vi told Victor, stepping back. Her mind was finally falling into focus. "We want every private eye that Ham respects working for us. Pay them whatever they want to starting right now. I need to know every single person Theo was blackmailing or had manipulated out of money in the last...at least three years."

Victor nodded.

"We also want every single person that was here looked into. At first superficially, but more deeply as needed. We need an overlap of names. Those are the likeliest suspects with the entirety of that Roche family at the head of the list."

"Good idea."

"We need Denny diving into all that gossip with that way of his. He gets people to tell him things because they think he's too stupid to realize what they're giving up. We want Papa looking into the elder crowd. He'll know who would actually disown a child or prevent a wedding and who wouldn't. Father will help, won't he?"

"Father likes Jack," Victor said, "and Father can make anything look like a conspiracy against Jack once we have the truth. Father can use all his connections to manipulate public opinion and the press *for* Jack."

"Dishonorable," Vi muttered, but she'd take it. She'd take whatever she could for Jack, even purchased press articles if that was what it took for them to tell the truth about her soon-to-be husband.

"Whatever it takes, Vi," Victor told her. She didn't disagree, so she simply nodded. Whatever it took indeed. It was too late to get started that evening other than collecting names and maybe sending hand-delivered notes to the private detectives' residences.

Violet pressed her hand to her forehead. "I have a lot to do."

"You need to talk to Jack and maybe even look at him," Victor told her.

"I didn't want to cry in front of everyone."

"You have to do it, Vi. It can't wait."

She nodded.

"He can take your tears."

Vi bit down on her bottom lip, afraid that he'd think she was crying over what was lost instead of the battle ahead.

"Vi," Victor said, taking hold of her arm and turning her to him, making him see her gaze. "Jack *wants* your tears and your worries. If you keep them from him, you start to scupper your marriage *before* you even get started."

"Does Kate tell you that stuff?"

"She taught me to tell her, love. You need Jack's worries too, love. Make sure he tells you."

Violet's eyes pooled with tears, but she wasn't ready to let them go, not really. So she just nodded and found her way back to the boudoir. Next door was the room she'd shortly be sharing with Jack. She sat down at her desk and started pulling her jewelry off, setting it onto the tray in front of her vanity. Pearls, bangles, earbobs, headpiece.

Everything except her engagement ring.

CHAPTER TEN

"What are you looking for, Violet?" Jack asked from the doorway of her bedroom at Victor's house.

She glanced away from the window. She'd been staring up at the sky where nothing but the moon shone through the pollution and she'd been wondering if that was all that was going to be left of her dreams. Stars that no one would ever see.

She nibbled at her bottom lip, which had gotten rather bruised from all the times she'd bit down on it to prevent a more extreme reaction to the evening. "I don't know."

His gaze was too penetrating as usual, and she didn't have the press of bodies and suspicions to hide behind anymore. She could hear her brother in her head. *Talk to him.*

"Are you angry?" Jack asked. His tone was carefully neutral.

Bloody hell, she thought, trying to keep her face blank. Was she angry? Of course she was! She was furious. She was 'shake her fist in the face of God' angry. She was furiously, blasphemously, *brokenly* angry. She was so angry it hurt. She was so angry she felt like a cracked vase a breath from falling to pieces. She was all of those things.

Rage was an ache in her stomach, acid in her throat. It was a burning in her heart and in her eyes, and she knew it wasn't his fault.

Her eyes welled with tears again, and she nodded. She didn't have the words to put to her emotions. Not when the fury was a tide that carried along with it terror of broken dreams, desperate, longing love, horrible fear that crafting the perfect beginning for their lives meant that they would lose all their chances at happiness.

"Do you want me to leave?"

She shook her head frantically, trying to find some way to convey her thoughts. They were too complex for sheer words. There was experience and hopes and dreams and fears and love, such deep abiding love, all wrapped up in her feelings.

He sat down in the deep, cushioned chair near the fire and watched her. She shifted on the window seat in her pajamas and kimono. Barefaced, dry-eyed, and chilled at the distance between them.

Their gazes were locked together, seemingly trying to speak to each other telepathically and unable to link their minds and hearts.

Slowly, Jack opened his arms. Vi whimpered at the sight of his wide arms, and she *flew* across the carpet and leapt into them. He hugged her so hard that she was crushed, and nothing had ever felt better. She trembled against him and realized he was shaking too. He was speaking, but she heard only the rushing of her blood and the pounding of his heart against her chest.

Finally, he stopped speaking and just rubbed her back, humming under his breath. Her trembling had stopped, and she felt as though it were possible to speak without crying. The case against him was strong, she knew. Together, they were stronger.

"Your family is going to be upset," Jack said. "My father is already in town, but I sent a boy over with a note. He'll be upset too, of course, but..."

"He won't think it's a good time to finally rid himself of you." Violet wound their fingers together. "Lady Eleanor will be by sooner or later crowing about how she was right about you, and it's time to flee to America or Greece or somewhere else."

"How are we going to do this, Vi? I know you didn't want to cry earlier, but why do I feel like you're mad at me? Is it Em?"

"Don't call her that to me," Violet told him. "No, it's not Emily. Was I upset that I found out the details of your life with her as they were shouted across our party? Yes. But, I could have guessed if I'd bothered to wonder about it."

"Then why am I in trouble?"

"I'm not mad at *you.*" She trailed her finger along his chest, watching the press of her nail against his evening clothes to avoid looking at his gaze, but he knew her too well for that.

Jack pressed his finger under her chin and slowly tilted her face to his. "Who has raised your ire?"

"The world," Violet snapped, letting out all the rage she was trying to hold back. "Theo, Roche, Algie, Victor, you, me, God himself. I want to shake my fist at the heavens, stomp my feet, have a good cry, and then pelt everyone with a rock. We're good people, aren't we?"

Jack nodded, and he whispered against her forehead before he pressed a kiss on her temple. "You are."

"I try to be good. I take care of orphans. I give to worthy causes. I hire former soldiers. I don't take advantage of the poor with my money. *Why* is this happening to us? Why are we so close to happiness only to have it yanked away? Why do I feel like we were so close this morning and now there's an abyss—"

Jack cut off Vi with a fervent kiss to her lips that didn't end for quite some time and left her both breathless and trembling. "There's no abyss we can't cross, Vi. Not as long as we're together."

She curled into his lap. "I'm just angry," she whispered.

"I can deal with angry or woebegone. As long as you're still mine."

"Always," Vi swore, hoping she wasn't causing that same mischievous sprite to test her resolution once again. She told him her plan while she sat with him in her bedroom. The door was open, and she could tell that despite the risk to their ever-after, Jack wasn't going to let whoever killed Theo ruin the plans he'd already laid out.

When they came together finally, it wasn't going to be because they were afraid they'd never get the chance. Violet hid a flash of disappointment as they took to her bed, and she let him hold her despite still wearing his evening clothes. They slept in each other's arms, and they both woke with a resolution to chip away at the crime until it was left in nothingness.

"Are we expecting your stepmother this morning?"

"Gerald should be able to buy us a day," Violet told Jack, pressing a kiss to his face before snuggling back down and breathing him in. She luxuriated in his arms, swearing she'd never take moments like these for granted again. It had become her life so quickly she'd forgotten there had been a time she'd woken alone and scared from nightmares every night. Violet pushed herself to a sitting position.

She had a lot to do to today and she suspected Jack had even more. He squeezed her hand before he left to change clothes. Violet dressed with Beatrice running into the bedroom the moment Jack left.

"They're delivering what you asked for now, my lady. I've got everything you need, I think. Mr. Carlyle was up early and he's already appearing with blokes in hand. They're having breakfast while they wait for you."

Violet nodded, leaving behind all but her engagement ring again. She was dressed for business in a grey sailor-style dress with grey stockings and sturdy shoes. She felt as though she could go for a long ramble or sit through a business meeting, and she really had no idea what the day was going to lay before her.

Violet hurried down the stairs and found Victor stepping out of the breakfast room.

"Darling devil, I'll have Hargreaves bring a tray to the parlor, shall I? Jack is talking to the blokes we've brought in."

"Is he telling them to do what it takes or to obey all laws?"

"The latter," Victor said with a wicked grin. "I made it clear I was paying them, and I expected results whatever the cost."

"Favorite brother." Vi tucked her arm through his elbow. "How are Kate and Violet Junior?"

"Vi Junior has taken it easier on her mother." Victor's lips twitched. "Kate's feet are mostly back to normal. She's still decided to curl up in bed with her feet propped up until she's needed."

Violet winced and then admitted, "I might need her to take on Lady Eleanor."

Victor paused and their gazes met. His mouth twisted. "I suppose one of us must. I have another idea, but it's evil."

"I'll do whatever it takes," Violet told him.

"Isolde is expecting."

Violet froze, staring at him. It *would* be quite evil to reveal Isolde's status as an expectant mother to distract her mother. However, if there was anything that could get Lady Eleanor to abandon all consideration of Vi or Victor, it was Lady Eleanor's children.

"Isolde might help us out on her own."

Victor's head cocked. "I'll take care of it. One way or the other. We'll get rid of Lady Eleanor until this is over."

Violet nodded and left him to go to the parlor. Beatrice was there and waiting. She'd already taken Violet's list of people she'd made last night and combined it with the guest list and the list from the police. The names of the people had been transcribed onto the eight chalk-boards that had been delivered that morning.

Violet walked along the list of names, reading over them and thinking of what she knew. "How many are there?" Violet asked.

"Eighty-seven," Beatrice replied.

Violet nodded. "How many didn't have someone else account for their whereabouts the evening before?"

"Sixteen."

"What about those on the guest list that weren't there when the police arrived."

"Nine more," Beatrice said softly. She had been taking typing classes and helping Violet with far more than her gowns in the last few months. Beyond that, she was naturally clever. Violet didn't need to explain twenty-seven names and four days before her wedding. The honeymoon and the wedding *could* be moved, but she was very much afraid that if they weren't able to find the truth by then, they'd never find it at all.

Possibly, very possibly, by using the very powerful people they could employ and the best defenses available, they'd be able to keep Jack out of jail, let alone the hangman's noose. But he'd never work again for Scotland Yard, and he'd be plagued by rumors. It would chase even their children.

CHAPTER ELEVEN

"Oh," Denny gasped, eyes wide and spinning as he took in the room with the chalkboards, the lists of names, the board with motives listed and room for names under each of the most common reasons for murder. "It's like all the dreams I didn't know to dream have come true." He glanced at the six private detectives, Ham, Jack, and then shook his head. He whispered loudly, "They're so serious."

"Take a seat, my lad," Lila told him dryly. "Try to contain your joy."

"Violet," Denny amended, "I am only semi-joyful. If anyone else were the main suspect, I'd be giddy. I admit it. I swear I'm appropriately serious. Jack, you believe me, don't you?"

Jack just lifted his brows and sipped his coffee. His mask was in full play, and he was enigmatically silent.

Violet glanced around the room, surprised that Jack and Ham weren't trying to take over, but she realized that Ham couldn't—not and maintain an ethical hand on the case in Scotland Yard. Jack, on the other hand, trusted her.

She stood and met everyone's gazes. Kate and Victor were sitting at the back of the room. Jack and Ham were at the front, side-by-side. They'd been discussing matters quietly. Rita had arrived and was near the corner, ready to aid in whatever was necessary. Gerald had sent a

note saying he would take care of Lady Eleanor for the day, but the earl
had arrived. He sat at the very back of the room next to Rita and
watched Violet expectantly. With Lila and Denny sitting near the
refreshments and Beatrice at the ready, nearly every single person
Violet trusted and loved was in the room ready to help her, along with
several private detectives they'd hired and her own man of business and
his assistant.

"You've all been apprised of the circumstances. We're working from
the absolute surety that Jack did not kill Theo. If you can't work
towards helping us to prove that, you need to leave now."

No one left.

"Lovely." Violet smiled woodenly and then turned to her man of
business. "We're also on a timeline, gentlemen and ladies. Jack and I
are supposed to get married on Saturday. I realize that's only three days
if you count today, and we're counting every minute."

There was a little shuffling, but Violet ignored it and glanced
around the room. Her gaze landed on her man of business. "Mr. Fred-
ericks, can you peel apart Theo's finances? Using connections and
whatnots?"

He paused. No doubt what she was asking was a rather unethical
endeavor, but when she waited, he nodded.

"Whatever you can find, please. Whatever staffing you need to use.
Whatever extra pay is necessary. We need to know, if possible,
everything."

"I'll try," he said. "If it can be found, I'll find it."

She nodded and turned to the rest of the group. "These are the
names," Violet told them. "People who were invited or we saw after the
party. That doesn't mean someone didn't crash our party, leave just
after Jack dragged Theo out, and not come back."

"It only takes a moment to murder someone if you know what
you're doing," one of the private investigators said. "Someone could
have easily murdered Smythe-Hill in a moment and come back inside,
joining the party and deliberately ensuring they were seen."

"There could be a faux-alibi in that mix of names," a man with a
missing arm agreed, gesturing with his remaining hand to the boards
with the entirety of all the names from all the lists. "There's also the

chance that the victim was thrown out by Mr. Wakefield and returned to meet someone for a previously arranged assignation."

Violet nodded. She didn't disagree at all and those options were haunting her. "That's why we're going to lay Theo's life bare and know his every secret by the time this is done. We're starting with the names here."

"Vi," Jack said, "the local boys make notes of things. They take note of who goes where. This street is well-protected. The local bobby is a good man, and he does his job well. He'd have noticed who was going where. Even with the party, if we can narrow down the list for him, he can help us."

"That's a job for the police," Ham cut in. "They'll do all they can to cover that angle. You can be assured that I'll be riding the detective and his team hard. They won't mess things up. You boys aren't here for that," he told the private detectives.

They really weren't, Vi thought. She glanced at the private detectives. "Which one of you is the most likely to break the rules?"

They stared at her in silence. A couple of them shifted and a few glances were tossed among themselves as if they were assessing each other, but no one spoke a word.

"Ham and Jack will forget the answer after this case, and for this case—it's what I'm looking for."

They were silent for a moment longer, then a slender, golden man raised his hand. "I'll be as disreputable as you need, my lady."

Vi nodded and glanced at the others. "Do any of you disagree that he'll be disreputable?"

The only answers were a sarcastic snort and a few head shakes. Lila laughed and rose. She started making notes on the board.

"You're kind of pretty for being a rogue," Vi told the disreputable private detective, who was grinning widely. She grinned back and Jack shifted. Violet ignored him. He had little real cause for jealousy, but if he wanted to be possessive in front of the devil who looked like an angel, Violet would be Jack's willing audience.

"Delightful," Violet told the angel-devil. "Your job is to take Theo's private life apart in all the ways. Break into his rooms, his friends' rooms, his enemies' rooms, his club. If you need snooty clothes, raid my brother's closet. If you need help getting into the clubs, Denny or Victor will take you. Dig, break, steal, whatever you need to do. You're not going to trace any of these leads, you're coming at the case from the other side. Find every sign of every person who might have hated or loved Theo enough to murder him."

The angel-devil shifted and his grin widened. She lifted her brows in question and he said, "So few realize that you kill who you love as much as who you hate."

"Sadly," Violet told them all, "this is not my first experience with murder."

He gave her a quizzical glance. She cared little if she was a puzzle to him as long as he worked on discovering all of Theo's secrets.

"Find every single enemy he had, every person he might have been blackmailing, and utterly disregard the law."

"Violet," Jack warned, leaning forward.

Vi ignored him and met the angel-devil's gaze. "Name?"

"John Smith," he said.

Vi's lips twitched. "Of course it is. Keep in touch with Victor. Ham won't tell you to break the law, and Jack will tell you not to. Victor doesn't care. I want a full picture of Theo's life. If you can get it to me in less than a day—and it's accurate—I'll pay you extra. Send me anything relevant the moment you find it."

Denny laughed. "Violet darling, you are my favorite." He rose and joined his wife, taking his own piece of chalk and adding his own notes. They were working on two of the eight chalkboards.

Smith nodded and she lifted a brow. "Go. You don't need to be here for the rest of this."

Violet turned to the others. "We have twenty-seven names that don't have easy alibis. We're starting there, but so will Scotland Yard. I don't care what the Yard knows. We need to know if any of these folks might have had a reason to kill Theo and if any of them has an alibi we don't know about. We need this list manageable. All of you send information as you have it. We don't have time to delay."

Violet had Beatrice hand out the lists to four of the remaining detectives. The lists included what they knew of the names, such as addresses, family, and rumors. They left a moment later.

There was but one investigator left. Ham had told her that Davey Milton was former military police. With his missing arm, he wasn't able to work for the Yard. She met his gaze, and he met hers without hesitation.

"Did you know Jack in the war?"

Milton nodded, a quick formal thing.

"Do you think he killed Theo?"

"Under the circumstances I heard?" He shook his head. "Never."

"You're Ham's man. Do whatever he thinks needs doing that Ham can't do himself. It'll be the stuff he can't assign to the Yard. Is that acceptable to you?"

Ham and Milton left, Ham speaking quietly to the last investigator. Violet took in a shaky breath. She'd saved herself the Roches, but she wasn't going to be able to leave the house without speaking to her father.

Would he support her and Jack or would he try to get her to leave Jack? A century ago, she wouldn't have been given a choice. Her gaze met his but his expression was unreadable. She glanced at Jack and then back at her father. Jack nodded. They would do this together—whatever it was.

"We'll help Denny and Lila narrow down and sort what we've learned so far on the people who were present. We need to put it all together and get rid of all the useless chaff." Violet glanced and saw that Lila had completely crossed out some names while other names—regardless of alibis—were receiving motives and details.

"I'm going to call my sister in," Lila said. "Some of these names here are in her set, including this fellow, Lyle Longfellow. Martha has spent rather a frequent evening with Lyle and his friends, and she was there last night. She won't lie, and I can pin her down on some of these fellows."

Violet winced, but she'd do whatever was necessary. Victor, however, groaned. Martha had once thrown herself at him with an eye on his fortune. Since that day, she still seemed to think she had a chance with Victor even though he was married.

Violet crossed to her father and leaned down to kiss his cheek. "Hello, Father. I'm glad you came."

Father waited for a long moment, his gaze passing back and forth. "Your stepmother thinks that I should put my noble foot down and demand you end this *ridiculous* engagement and save yourself and our family name."

"Interesting," Violet told him, flatly. Her tone and expression made her thoughts clear.

Father smiled gently, but his eyes were apologizing already for what he had to say. "Violet..." Combined with his gaze, her father's tone told her all she needed to know about where he stood. She glanced at Jack and saw his jaw flex—he'd seen the same as she.

Her heart clenched.

"I didn't kill Smythe-Hill, sir," Jack said. He might as well have been commenting on the weather.

"I don't doubt that," her father replied. "Choices, however, must be made. This is an interesting operation and one I hope works. Yet, you could fail. If you don't find the killer, the world will blame Jack regardless. That's not..."

Violet met her father's gaze. She'd never realized until that moment that she and Victor had their father's eyes. In every other way, they took after their mother. Vi hoped that with matching eyes, he'd see her utter rejection of what he was about to say.

"Violet," Father said again, more firmly. "Hard choices must be made. Your stepmother and I are concerned about your life and your happiness if Jack isn't exonerated. There's more than just this moment to think of, you realize. There's yourself, your children, your siblings, our name. Geoffrey still has his life to create. He's in school where things are hard with a suspected murderer in the family. Gerald isn't married yet. The right young women won't marry into a family with a killer."

Violet slowly rose. "Father, the entirety of my life you have chosen everyone else but Victor and I. You handed us to Aunt Agatha—and looking back, I'm grateful. But you still handed us over. I don't remember Peter and Lionel's faces because I so rarely saw them."

Father blinked, starting to speak, but Violet didn't let him. She was *not* finished.

"I won't lie and say that I don't care what you choose, and I suppose I won't be surprised if you don't choose me once again. It turns out that when it comes right down to it, I know who my family is." She glanced at Lila and Denny carefully making notes on the chalk-boards. At Rita who knew far less of those names than the others, but Vi knew that Rita would do what she could. She glanced at Kate and Victor, and finally at Jack. "I won't abandon the man I love for the wants of a stepmother who doesn't even like me, a father who has never made me a priority, a wart of a younger brother who is already half-ruined by your wife. Isolde is already happy, and I have little doubt she won't abandon me or Victor. Gerald is a rich, future earl. Notoriety will just make him more interesting."

"Violet!" Father snapped—too loud—because everyone turned their way. "There are matters you aren't considering."

"No," Violet hissed back, winding her fingers through Jack's. "Father, I have loved you despite the way you tossed Victor and me aside—"

"You were happier with Agatha. The first visit was to just get a handle on your grief. A change of scenery," Father said, voice cracking. "I didn't want you to go. My God, I adored your mother. I miss her daily. I see her in your face, and it kills me every time. Despite all that, I'd have wanted nothing more than to watch every second of your life. Only you were happier *with* Agatha. You blossomed. Agatha was magical with you. I didn't throw you away; I *let you go.*"

"There's no scenario where I leave Jack," Violet told her father precisely. "Even if he is arrested, even if they..." Violet couldn't finish the statement, but Jack pressed her hand as if he knew that losing him would demolish whatever happiness this life could have provided.

"Did you really adore our mother?" Victor asked quietly. None of them had noticed him approaching.

"If I could have given my life for hers, I would have," their father said, glancing between them as if surprised by the question. "I would have given my kingdom, all that I had, save my children, to save her. Even now, just for a day with her, I'd give up all I have. I didn't know. I didn't realize you didn't know that. I should have realized you had no idea. How could you?"

Victor shook off the answer, even though both of them were

snatching up the words and hiding them inside of their hearts. "Then you have a perfect understanding of how Violet feels, Father. You wouldn't have abandoned our mother. Violet won't abandon Jack. The only choice to be made is yours. We—" Victor gestured to himself, Vi, Jack, Kate, and the baby. "We've already chosen."

Father leaned back. "Vi..."

She wasn't capable of speech at that moment. She was trying her hardest to hold on to her emotions until after Jack was free. This... whatever this was...it wasn't helping.

The earl glanced among all of them and deflated. Whatever superior air that had been fed to him with his mother's milk faded and all that was left was a man. Their father, who was half a stranger, never seemed so far lost to them than when he realized that they *would* choose Jack. No matter the cost that the earl exacted, they would choose Jack every time.

The earl took in a deep breath with a shudder. "I—" He paused, glancing among them, and then he said something Violet wouldn't have expected. "I always liked you for Violet, Jack. Eleanor hates the sheer idea of you, but Violet isn't Isolde, who would fall in love with any man who needed her. You don't bore Vi. You protect her. She writes her books and drags you to Cuba. She has her parties and you dance with her despite the roller skates. She's happier when you're around."

Jack shifted a little, as did Victor, but Violet was frozen. She hadn't realized her father knew about their roller-skate parties. She hadn't realized he'd taken note of how much she loved to write. She hadn't realized—she'd never even realized herself until that moment—that she had been bored by those who had tried to pursue her before. She'd had *no idea* that her father knew her so very well. Her eyes were burning with tears again, and she bit down hard on her poor, bruised bottom lip as her father smiled gently at her.

"I'm sorry." He met her gaze when he said it, and his voice was clear and even. "I never should have let Eleanor convince me." He ran his hands over his thinning hair. "This isn't an easy road, Violet. I only want to protect you. It's what parents want to do even when it's the wrong thing."

Violet glanced at Jack, and he said so very gently, "Believe him. If I thought you'd leave me, I'd try to convince you to. I want the easier road for you too."

Violet's gaze widened, and her mouth dropped.

"Your father is right, Vi. If I'm not exonerated, the whispers will never stop."

She started to tell him she didn't care, but he stopped her by cupping her cheek and letting his thumb run along her bottom lip.

"I know," he told her. "I know you won't leave me. We might be very different creatures, Vi, but at our hearts, we're the same. I wouldn't leave you either, and leaving you will never be the easier road for me. Never."

"Never," she swore. "*Never!*"

CHAPTER TWELVE

"Where's your father?" the earl asked Jack, once Violet finally looked away.

"He's buying the press, I believe," Jack admitted, flushing. "Leading them to report on the kind of man Theo was rather than on the suspect at hand. He says he doubts it'll work for long."

Violet's father nodded, and to her utter shock Father stood and his hand snaked out to pull her against his chest. "Someone killed Theo. We'll find the man."

Violet stood stiffly in her father's arms for a moment before she relaxed and hugged him back before escaping to Jack.

The earl excused himself a few minutes later, muttering, "Wakefield isn't the only man with connections to flex."

"What are you doing, Father?" Violet asked.

"Never you mind," he said. "These are the types of things you don't admit to doing."

Violet pressed herself against Jack the moment her father left. She was shuddering, holding on to all of her emotions, which were in a cyclone, and she didn't have time for it.

"Are you all right, my love? That was intense, and he isn't even my father."

Violet nodded a lie and then pulled away. Time to focus on other things. She could have sleepless nights wondering if her father really had adored her mother. If he really had let her and Victor go *because* of love rather than the lack of it. To wonder if he'd watched her from afar, loving her the entire time, and somehow forgetting to help her see.

Violet physically shook off her thoughts, pressed a kiss on Jack's jaw, and then crossed to the chalkboards where Lila was muttering instructions and flipping through the pages of notes from the interviews the police had conducted the day before.

"What have you done?" Violet asked, gesturing to the board where Lila and Beatrice were making notes and Kate was reading through the stack of what they had uncovered so far.

"While your father did the expected and then the very unexpected?" Denny asked, almost bouncing on his toes. "That moment was a....it was a thing of beauty. Better than any play. I was reeling, darling one. Simply reeling. When we weren't knocked sideways? We were—ah —darting glances at one another, biting our tongues, dying to speak, manfully holding back exclamations of shock and awe."

Violet rubbed her forehead, wondering why she liked Denny as much as she did. "With the names, of course, you nitwit."

"These ones that are crossed out," Lila answered, elbowing her husband aside, "they're the names of people that I'm certain didn't kill Theo."

"How certain?"

"Very," Lila said clearly.

Violet waited, gesturing for Lila to explain. There could be no mistakes.

Lila nodded, understanding. "They really do have good alibis. For example, Helen Nathans, who was absolutely chasing Paul Lansing the entire evening. They both claimed to be together in their separate interviews with the police." Lila flipped to the notes that Beatrice had transcribed the night before. "Helen would have very definitely noticed if Paul had left even for a few moments. He alibied her as well, but *he* might not have noticed if she disappeared."

Denny scoffed. "He was trying to shake her loose. He was with that married couple who strays on each other constantly."

Lila nodded. "Helen did say that for the time period after Jack left, she and Paul had been speaking with Amelia and Nigel Banks. As Amelia steps out on Nigel and Paul was an easy conquest who would have welcomed such a dalliance, you can be assured that Helen was *well* aware of exactly where Paul and Amelia were for the whole of the evening. With that backstory and the agreeing but separate statements to the police, I think we can be sure they didn't kill Theo. Besides, a couple who strays like that isn't an easy mark for blackmail. Everyone knows what they've been up to, and the two of them don't care. Helen's money is secured, and she'd never fall for Theo's nonsense. She's way too straight-forward for Theo. Paul would absolutely end up in Theo's clutches, but he has three people agreeing on his whereabouts during the murder."

"Darling love, chocolate of my heart," Denny said, nuzzling Lila's cheek, "you've a little Violet Carlyle in you right now."

Lila rolled her eyes and ignored Denny. "I've crossed a lot of those names off. Just cleaning up who we don't need to worry about. We'll need to find those like Garfield Ives who is quiet fellow and he says he was refilling his plate. No one would have noticed that except a servant. Ives is too quiet and easily overlooked. If someone did notice him, they'd have avoided him. You didn't even invite him, Vi. He came with Herbert Miles, who keeps Ives around because Ives is flush and Miles gets farther by getting Ives to pay."

"Ouch," Kate said. "Is that really how it is for Ives? The poor lad. We should be friends with him after all this."

"Oh no," Lila shook her head, "he might be easily overlooked and pitiful, but he's also a right wart. I've seen more than one of the girls slap him a new one when he let his hand stray."

Kate's gaze narrowed and she sniffed. "Please disregard my previous statement."

"I think I can go through all of this and get you a secondary list. It'll whittle out the dead weight of everyone we're concerned might seem to have an alibi but probably doesn't, really. Beatrice, Kate and I can work together. Double check those with alibis, make a list of people we should double check the validity of their statements and those we can bypass. Like the servants for Ives. I assume you and Jack are bearding the Roches?"

"Yes. Algie suggested we save them for a day or two. They're being scoured by the Yard at the moment. We need them when they aren't being watched quite so closely."

"They were being blackmailed and none of them have alibis," Lila said. "I looked them up first. Mr. Roche the elder said he was drinking in the library and didn't know anything was wrong until after the police arrived. Barty and Gertrude had a bit of a spat, and Barty said he was in the ballroom, but no one verifies that. Gertrude said she went to the ladies, but again, no one verified that. Clara's brother, Robbie, said he stepped out for a smoke in the garden, but he was near the hydrangea. He didn't see anything and said there were a few others out there smoking. No names or even faces due to the darkness."

Violet rubbed the back of her neck. "They were getting pressed by Theo. Barty was at real risk of losing money. They're the reason why Theo was even at the party. All of them are primary suspects. Even Gertrude since only Algie and Clara have alibis."

"The police will be looking to them too," Jack said, "I doubt Detective Clarkson will be happy to find us there before him."

"Oh," Rita piped in. "Jimmy's going to ring up the house after the Yard leaves. The Yard detective arrived as I left the hotel."

Violet grinned. "You brilliant thing. What have you done?"

"Hotel Saffron takes its guests' desires very seriously," Rita told them. "It's quite a bit better than living in a regular house. They've risen to a whole other level given that I took my room indefinitely. I am quite...spoiled? I'm not even sure that's the right word. I thought I was spoiled before, but I didn't know the meaning until they taught me. I'm a princess from kingdom Saffron."

Violet laughed at the look of semi-awe on Rita's face.

"Also," Rita told them, "I quite like most of the staff. I spoke with Mr. Yardley today. He runs the hotel. He's using the staff to find out what he can about the Roches and Theo. I was shocked, but I suppose an indefinitely-present guest trumps the temporary ones."

"I would lay a fiver on the Roches having tried to bully their way into your penthouse suite, Rita," Denny said gleefully, rubbing his hands together with joy. "I bet they made an enemy and haven't even realized it."

Vi closed her eyes in relief. Having the hotel servants on their side, if one of the Roches were the killer, could be the ace they needed to win this game.

～

"This is going better than I thought it would," Jack said as he tugged Violet up the steps to her bedroom. They walked inside of the room, and he shut the door, turning her so she was pressed against the wood. Somehow his warmth surrounding her made her shiver, and she leaned her forehead into his chest, breathing slowly. It wasn't even time for luncheon, and she felt as though she were a dishrag used to scrub the stairs and wrung out dozens of times.

"Do you think we can do this?"

"We have private investigators who are actually good at what they do being promised untold amounts of money to deliver. We have ins with staff at the hotel, with the press, with Scotland Yard, even with lords and brilliant men of business, all working for us."

Violet didn't look up. She heard the edge of hope in his voice and hadn't realized that he hadn't been feeling it until it came back. The dawning of his hope was making hers all the more fragile. Perhaps she hadn't realized *quite* how bad things were—and she'd been well aware that it wasn't good.

"Is that a yes?" Violet finally dared to whisper.

Jack turned her face up to his and kissed her lightly on the forehead, the nose, and each cheek before rubbing his jaw over the top of her head. "Yes. If it can be done, I think we'll be able to do it."

Violet couldn't hold back the trembling then. She bit down hard on her lip as though she could hide her feelings. She couldn't. His gaze was far too penetrating for that. She tried closing her eyes, but that wouldn't work either. He didn't need her eyes to read her emotions. Not when he had her hands, her mouth, the feel of her trembling, all the little asides of the day, the sure understanding of each moment of the day and how they'd built to bring her here.

"I don't know what to do now," Violet confessed. "What do we do?"

Jack kissed each of her closed eyelids. "It's possible we've done all we could until we have more information."

"We should be reading the notes from the police interviews," Violet told him. "We should be...I don't know...cross-examining the servants or searching the bushes or—"

Jack's laugh broke into Violet's rambling, and she scowled up at him.

"This is serious." She wriggled to get away from him, but he didn't let her go.

"I know," he told her seriously, but his lips were twitching as he did.

"I could search bushes," Violet sniffed.

"You'd be writing treatises on it, in no time."

Violet would have tried to elbow him, but there was a knock on her door and Beatrice called out. "My lady? Kate would like your assistance with some of the paperwork we're going through."

"Oh no!" Jack grinned. "The future treatise on searching bushes is lost."

Violet did elbow him then. She crossed to her armoire and took out a grey jumper to go with her grey dress. The wind had picked up, the skies were darkening with a spring storm, and Violet hoped it wasn't an indication of things to come.

Before she left her bedroom, Jack took her face between his palms and kissed her into near senselessness. She took every caress willingly and gave him her own. Both of them were too well aware that if all fell apart and their friends weren't able to help as much as they hoped, Jack might well spend the rest of his days paying for a crime he didn't commit.

The next two days passed in a blur of reports from private detectives, articles about Jack's work and the 'frame-up' job being cast the honorable former military man. The angel-devil detective learned so much about Theo that Violet felt certain he could strip any person bare of their secrets simply by being in the same room with him. Their list of suspects grew and shrank and with each passing hour, Violet was wound into a tighter and tighter coil until she felt that one stiff breeze might make her collapse into a cross between a tantrum and hysterics.

CHAPTER THIRTEEN

"You're Miss Rita's friend?" the elevator attendant asked Friday morning. Violet was supposed to be married the next day, and the question jerked Violet out of her thoughts about the likelihood of that event. Given Jack's tighter and tighter jaw and the way he stared into corners, Violet wasn't certain he had very much more faith in his ability to remain free than she did.

The elevator attendant nodded politely, but there was a bit of a twinkle in his gaze that distracted Vi. He was wearing a spiffy red uniform with shining shoes and etched name badge that read Cooper. Everything about him was perfectly precise, like all of the staff of Hotel Saffron. Even the maids, coming from the rooms they were just cleaning, seemed pressed and shined.

Vi nodded in answer with a quick wink. "Rita's rather a good friend." Violet had only known her for a few months but somehow they'd become nearly as close as Lila and Vi. The three of them were so very different, and yet, they had so very much in common.

In fact, Rita had left Victor's house and come with Violet and Jack to the hotel. Only, when they'd stepped into the grand lobby, Rita had stepped into the manager's office with a rather large box of treats.

"Mr. Yardley said to ensure you'd have anything you needed." The elevator attendant grinned wickedly. "Anything at all."

Jack cleared his throat. "What can you tell us about the Roches?"

He shifted a little as though speaking about them went against his better judgement. "They're a difficult crew except for Miss Clara and her English bloke. Mr. Roche the elder is demanding and difficult to please. Mr. Robbie is nice enough, but he disappears when everyone thinks he's in his room. Tends to step out the back and bribe his way back in."

"What about Barty and Gertrude?"

"She's a sour one. He's easy enough. Keep his bar stocked and lie to his fiancé when she goes looking for him, and he's well pleased. Tips rather generously, but he charges it to the rooms and Mr. Roche senior is paying for them, I believe."

The elevator had stopped and the attendant kept the door closed long enough to add, "It isn't just Mr. Robbie who steps out at night. Mr. Barty and Miss Gertrude do as well."

"Together?" Violet remembered that sour twist to Gertrude's mouth and found it hard to believe that she'd do much more than go to dinner in the evening. Perhaps to an upstanding play or symphony.

The attendant shook his head and glanced around even though they were in a confined space. "She leaves a few minutes after Mr. Barty does—sometimes in the breath of him—and after she's supposedly gone to her rooms. Sometimes she doesn't come back 'til the early morning."

"Does she take a black cab?"

"There's usually a car waiting for her."

"Close enough to Barty's exit that she's following him?" Jack asked, glancing at Violet.

The attendant shrugged. "It would be very possible certainly."

"Why wouldn't she hire someone to follow him rather than doing it herself? She's not from London. It would be easy to lose someone not knowing the city, and she has more than enough money for that if the rumors are true."

"Maybe she didn't want anyone to know what she was finding out," the attendant suggested. "I followed my girl once when she was step-

ping out on me. I needed to know who it was before I decided what
to do."

"Who was it?" Violet asked, temporarily distracted.

"My brother," the attendant replied, glancing at his feet.

"What did you do?"

"Broke things off. A few months later they were engaged. They
have a few little ones now."

"Does your brother know you know?" Violet asked him.

He shook his head, eyes crinkling for a moment. "Family isn't so
easily disposable—I was choosing my brother when I broke things off
with her."

"And you don't hate him?" Violet asked, searching his face.

"After they announced their engagement, he told me. Told me he
fell for her when she was with me, and he'd hated himself ever since.
He asked me to forgive him, and I did. Not too long later, I met my
wife. I thank God every day I followed her that day. If I'd gotten one
of my friends to do it, maybe my pride would have played a bigger part
than I wanted."

Violet reached out her hand and shook his. "You're a good man. It's
an honor to meet you."

They left the elevator and made their way to the Roche suite where
Mr. Roche senior and Clara were staying. Algie had rooms in the city,
but Violet had heard he basically was living at the hotel as well. Jack
knocked on the door while Violet fiddled with her engagement ring.

She wasn't sure what to do with the information they'd received,
and Jack had said nothing either. Were they going to confront
everyone who snuck out or have someone follow them and see what
they were up to? What if they discovered Barty simply going to jazz
clubs or parties? That was hardly useful information.

The door to the suite was opened by Algie, who met their gazes
and whispered, "Pretend I had nothing to do with you being here."

"You do have nothing to do with us being here," Violet told Algie.
"You are one of the few of this lot who has an alibi anyone believes."

Algie laughed nervously. "I suppose it helps that Clara and I were
with Isolde and Tomas. You wouldn't believe me otherwise."

"I would," Violet told him in a low voice, while someone from inside the suite asked who was at the door. It wasn't even a lie. Algie wasn't conniving enough to see Jack drag Theo out into the night and think, 'Now's the time to murder the lad.'

"Really, Algie darling, who is it?" Clara peeked over Algie's shoulder and her gaze widened. "Father said they'd come now that a body was tossed into their laps."

"Does he still want our help?" Jack asked, squeezing Violet's fingers.

So they were going to ask their questions that way.

"Why would I need it?" Roche demanded loudly. "The fiend is dead."

"So," Violet said lightly, "you've recovered the blackmail proof?"

Roche harrumphed. "Let them in, lad. Clara duckling, you really could do so much better than this fool."

Algie's ears turned red, but he just smiled jovially.

"Papa," Clara shot a daggered glare at her father. "If I wanted to marry someone like you, perhaps. That's not what I want."

Roche just shook his head as though it wasn't insulting and muttered, "You'll learn eventually, girl. Algie will get you in trouble, and you'll have to call on your old father. Maybe I won't rescue you. You know I believe in reaping what you sow."

"We'll help though," Violet told him. "You might be all that Clara has, but Algie is rather rich in family."

Roche harrumphed again and crossed his arms over his chest. "I bet you wish you'd helped us before Smythe-Hill died. I admit I'm surprised you're not behind a barred door, Wakefield."

Jack didn't take up the gauntlet that Roche was throwing down. Violet found she wasn't all that surprised that Roche was petty. She'd love to see him taken down a peg or two. Instead, she glanced around the suite. Only Roche, Algie, and Clara were present.

"Looking for the others?" Roche laughed sarcastically, completely unfeeling to their plight. "Gertrude dragged them off to the museum. She said Barty needed a little polish and Robbie could stand some as well. Not sure how she convinced Robbie to go, but go he did."

Algie winced at Violet's glance, but she said nothing. She was sure that he loved Clara, and Violet wouldn't have minded her if she came without her father. Instead she laughed merrily and mocked,

"Scotland Yard doesn't arrest the first person who comes along. They're looking for evidence. Since Jack didn't kill Theo, there *isn't* any."

"Is that what your lover and your affable dragon told you? They're just trying to avoid your hysterics, m'dear."

Violet's gaze narrowed. "Careful now. We know the secret you're so careful to keep from Gertrude, and I don't care if your nephew successfully sucks her into his marriage trap. How long do you think it will take before he's stepping out on her and not even trying to hide it? Whatever will she do then?"

"Violet," Jack said, placing a hand on her arm. He smiled a snake's smile at Roche that Violet had never seen before. "Settle down, love."

Algie's gaze widened, almost panicked as he stared at Violet, waiting for her to explode. Instead she fluttered her lashes and glanced to the side to hide the ire that Jack would have deserved if he wasn't playing Roche.

"We both want the same thing," Jack told Roche. "We want to find out who killed Theo and why. Me because I don't want the crime pinned on me. You because you need whatever evidence Theo had on your nephew that might still be out there. He must have had something, right?"

Roche stared at Jack for a moment and then nodded very slightly. "Some letters. Between him and me and Barty and that *girl* he married."

"It's both of our interest," Jack told Roche, glancing at Clara and Algie, "to have this wrapped up quickly. Algie is connected enough to Vi that the rumors will extend to him and your daughter. Gertrude is clearly suspicious. I was able to bribe one of the servants into admitting that she follows Barty sometimes when he leaves. He thinks she's secure in her room, and instead, she's keeping an eye on him. I wonder if he's already pushed her too far."

Violet gasped, eyes wide as if she didn't know. "I'd throw you over if you were stepping out on me," Violet told Jack. She glanced meaningfully to Roche. "As would any modern woman. We don't have to put up with the old ways. Especially when all the money is hers."

Roche was flummoxed, but Clara was staring at her feet.

"Did you know?" Violet asked Clara. Algie's brilliant blush told Violet what she needed to know.

"I didn't know where she was going," Clara finally said. "I thought I saw her one night, so I knocked on her door to check. She never answered. I stayed up and watched the front of the hotel, but I never saw her come in. She was, however, at breakfast, so I assume she slept through my knocking or she decided not to answer."

Clara was staring at her shoes again, and her pretty cheeks were blushing. Violet wasn't going to let her get away with a half a truth. "You don't think that's the case, though, do you?"

Clara didn't answer. Algie whispered something to her. Violet saw his mouth form the word, 'Please.' Roche didn't notice as he was too busy staring out the window, but his cheeks were flushed too.

Clara finally confessed. "We shared a cabin on the crossing. I don't think she could have possibly slept through me. She woke with every little sound. When she's tired, she's vicious."

"Was she vicious the next day?"

Clara met Violet's gaze and shook her head just the slightest.

"Did you know she was wandering around London on her own?" Jack asked Roche. "Surely her parents entrusted her safety to you."

"Of course I didn't!" Roche thundered. "I'm not convinced she was. She's a good girl. Maybe she didn't answer Clara's knocking because she didn't want to. It's not like she's obligated to run to the door every time someone knocks. I certainly don't. Clara even watched for Gertrude to come in and didn't see her. Yet she was at breakfast the next day."

Violet didn't see the point in arguing, so she glanced to Jack. Roche preferred the questions coming from him anyway.

"Where was Barty going?" Jack asked Roche.

He showed a flash of distinct anger. "He got sucked into some gambling. He's drawn to it like some are drawn to opium dens. No matter how many times I shout at him."

"Who pays his bills when he bets more than he has?"

"I don't," Roche thundered.

Vi noticed the flush on both Algie and Clara. Both of them carefully avoided Roche's gaze, and Vi did nothing more than nudge Jack's foot to ensure he saw what she saw.

"I wonder if he was gambling with Theo," Violet said. "Theo was good at getting you to play his games when you knew better, Algie."

"I stopped that a long time ago," Algie said. "Wouldn't know, but maybe I could find out."

"Do," Jack ordered. "In fact, take Denny with you. Denny and a friend of his. A John Smith. We'll send them over."

"Algie is dining with us at the Savoy," Roche said, shooting them a glance that dared them to counter his statement.

"Father," Clara snapped, "Algie is helping his family."

"Were you really in the library?" Violet asked Roche.

"I wouldn't have murdered that slug," Roche said. "I wasn't gonna pay his blackmail, I wasn't gonna put up with this attempt to romance my Clara, and I wasn't gonna go to jail for the blighter either."

Clara rose suddenly. "I need some air. Father, you know this is going over my and Violet's heads. We'll take a turn in the garden. Algie and Jack can come fetch us when you're done here."

Violet stood at Clara's declaration and put on her hat and coat. The two of them rode down in the elevator with the attendant carefully avoiding both of their gazes.

CHAPTER FOURTEEN

*V*iolet lifted her brows the moment they were alone in the gardens. There were lovely roses just starting to bloom, a gazebo, and even a pond with a few ducks. Violet wanted to visit when there were ducklings since she counted two mated pairs, but she did nothing more than wait for Clara to speak.

"Gertrude knew about the child," Clara said. "I told her. I told her that Barty had married once in the height of passion, lost his wife to childbirth, and had a little girl. I didn't tell her the rest. About the baby being Cuban or the gambling or the lost fortune. I think Barty told her that his own father lost the money in a series of bad investments before he died. Barty makes it all sound very tragic."

Violet paused. "Gertrude knew of the child and said nothing?"

"We were rather friendly until then. I talked about how sweet Maria is, how she's a little angel with a pretty voice, how much we loved her. How she needed a mama. Someone like Gertrude to love her and see to her. Gertrude told me she didn't want to raise some other woman's child, but she supposed a school could be arranged."

Clara nibbled on her thumbnail and then apologized for it. "Terrible habit, I know. I asked Algie if we could raise her." Her eyes filled with tears. "He didn't even think twice. He just said, of course, and ordered her the most elaborate dollhouse known to mankind. Then he sent for her himself, inviting her nanny, so she wouldn't be scared."

"Algie's a bit of a dimwit," Violet told Clara, who flashed a furious gaze towards Violet. "I'd rather have a man with his good heart, however, than Theo's wits. He'll make your happiness his goal for the rest of his days, and he'll love that little girl as though you placed her in his arms on the day of her birth."

"I haven't told Father I am not going to go back to America," Clara admitted after a moment. "I love my father, and I hate him at the same time. He's a good man and a terrible man. He loves me, and he's good to me, but he'll needle Algie until the day he dies and probably from the grave."

Violet didn't make a comment.

"I'm not giving him up," Clara said to the question Violet didn't ask. "We'll visit often. I just won't afflict Algie with Papa if I can help it."

"Does Barty mind you adopting his daughter?"

Clara's expression soured. "He should have cared more. He looked —" Clara grunted a little as if the answer pained her and then said, "relieved. He said he knew I'd take good care of her and he'd sign whatever I needed him to sign. We're waiting until after the wedding, but he won't change his mind."

"She's lucky to have you," Violet told her, "*and* Algie."

"She deserves more from her father," Clara snapped.

Violet rubbed her brow, thinking of her morning with her father. "My father let my aunt raise me and my twin. He said it was painful. That he loved us too much to keep us when we thrived with her. Tell her that. Tell her he wanted her happiness more than his own. Make *sure* she knows even if it's all lies." Violet paused. "Is Gertrude really not here?" she asked.

Clara nodded.

"And Barty and Robbie?"

Clara nodded again.

"I need to see their rooms," Violet told her. Her expression was pure daring.

Clara paused for long enough to make Violet wonder what she'd do if Clara didn't comply. Perhaps, she'd just bribe her way into a room or get Rita to do so. Clara took a deep breath and nodded. "I don't think any of them have anything to do this with the murder, but if it will get you closer to an answer, even if it is only to rule them out, I'll help."

Violet and Clara returned to the lobby where Clara got extra keys from the man at the desk with pretty lies and they made their way to the rooms.

"Barty's first," Clara said. "He'll be the hardest to appease if he gets back to the hotel first. I haven't particularly cared what Gertrude thought of me since she tossed aside Maria."

Violet didn't care whose room they searched first. She wanted to smirk at Jack and tell him that she'd get to search her bushes after all and write a treatise if she wanted, but she had a soon-to-be cousin along. Violet went straight to the desk, digging through the papers. She found a small, black book with names and addresses that were primarily female. At the sight, she lifted her brows. It had all kinds of small notes. Violet tucked it into her pocket without a modicum of regret.

She took a whole pile of personal letters as well, wrapping them up in brown paper from a package and then turned to Clara. The girl had looked under the bed, through all the drawers, and ran her hand behind the wardrobe.

"There's nothing that I can find. I went through his luggage too, but it's empty. I even felt for something in the lining, but you can tell there's nothing there."

"Does he have any books?"

Clara scoffed and shook her head. No pages to search then.

"Are you taking his personal letters?"

Violet nodded. Perhaps Clara deserved a bit of an explanation. "I'll do whatever is necessary to keep Jack free."

Clara just smiled wickedly. "I'd do the same for Algie."

"Then we're agreed."

Violet let Clara lead the way to Robbie's room, but as they opened the door, it was opened from the inside. Oh! Why hadn't they knocked first? Clara gasped and stepped back and then blinked in surprise at a man in a sharp black suit.

"Mr. Yardley?"

"Miss Roche," Mr. Yardley said. "Pardon me, ma'am. The maid noticed some damage, and I was just examining what needed to be done."

He lied smoothly, but Violet noted the maid behind him with twitching lips. Blonde marcelled waves, brilliant blue eyes, curvy frame, holding a basket behind her. Rita's and Violet's gazes met.

"Have you been to the fiancé's room yet?" Violet asked.

Rita shook her head as Mr. Yardley said, "I'm sure I don't know what you mean."

"Oh, it's all right, Mr. Yardley," Clara said. "I'm afraid we're up to the same hijinks. What if we shut this door and leave you to it, and you don't visit Miss Campbell's room?"

Mr. Yardley's expression never changed, keeping a perfectly calm expression even as he shut the door in Violet's and Clara's face.

"Did you find anything?" Violet whispered to Rita.

She shook her head. "Most of them except Clara and Mr. Roche senior leave when the rest think they're in bed. Gertrude gets in a regular car after Barty leaves. Robbie comes and goes as he wishes. He doesn't try to hide it. The other two bribe their way in and out back doors and pay servants to say they were in places they weren't."

"A regular car? How odd," Violet said. "She must have hired someone to take her about when she could be free of her fiancé."

"Let's toss Gertrude's room," Clara said and Violet winked a goodbye to both Yardley and Rita. This time, Clara knocked on the door and waited. There was no answer after a couple of minutes.

"I think we're clear to go in, dear."

"Mr. Yardley gave me such a turn," Clara whispered. "My hands are trembling still."

Violet took the key from Clara and unlocked the door. She called, "Housekeeping!" and waited for an answer that didn't come.

Violet hurried through digging in Gertrude's papers, finding nothing. Not a single paper, a single letter, nothing. She glanced away from the desk and found Clara strewing Gertrude's clothes about the room.

"This way," Clara said as she continued, careful to step on one of the finer nightgowns, "Barty will assume his things were rifled as well and for some reason they took his papers. He's not very bright, really. His need to gamble rides him like he's the pony instead of the man."

"It seems like a good reason to kill someone," Violet said, lifting her brow at Clara. "Do you think your cousin killed Theo?"

Clara didn't answer, and Violet turned up from where she was flipping through books to examine her cousin's fiancé. The girl was carefully avoiding Violet's gaze and shuffling through the drawers without really looking at anything.

"Do that more carefully," Violet told the girl, leaving the subject of Barty behind. Vi would ask about Robbie when she didn't need Clara's careful attention.

The two of them worked quickly, leaving the room a disaster with several things damaged just enough. Even with all of that, Violet didn't find one single thing in Gertrude's room that was worthy of note.

"Does she not get letters from friends and family?"

"She does."

Violet's mouth twisted as she glanced through the room again. There was utterly nothing. Then Violet sighed. "If there's anything to find it has to be in your suite. You'll need to search it. Have Algie invite your father to meet mine. Have him take along the lads and then send Gertrude away because you're ill."

"She'll just expect me to go to my room and she'll use the suite. The sitting room there really is more comfortable than our bedrooms for reading or writing letters."

"Then be rude," Violet ordered.

Clara winced. "For Algie, anything."

Violet didn't tell her the same, but yes, for Jack—anything. Including demanding a nice girl to be terribly rude to her near-brother's intended. Speaking of, Violet thought, glancing Clara over. "It's time for you to be a bit crueler to your Barty."

"I'm sure I don't know what you mean."

"Your father has made it clear that he won't finance Barty. If Papa Roche knew you were financing him, would he cut off your allowance?"

Clara flushed again, avoiding answering to avoid lying. Violet sighed. "Algie's inheritance is secure enough these days now that his father has paid off his debts, but Algie won't ever say no to your Barty as long as you want Algie to rescue him. Every time you do, you take money from little Maria and the children to come. They'll have to work and won't be able to follow their dreams while you support Barty in his *needs*."

Clara sniffed, biting her thumbnail again, and then she screwed up her face. "Robbie won't help Barty anymore, either. He never does pay you back even when he promises so faithfully."

"Just think of your children," Violet advised. "I know you love them already."

Clara's gaze met Violet's. "They become more concrete, don't they? When you've met their father and can anticipate their arrival. It's like I can see their ghosts, feel them haunting me, letting me know they're coming. Is that utterly mad?"

Clara's self-deprecating laugh didn't strike Violet as all that funny. Her own future children were haunting Violet too, making her think of how things would affect them if their father was a suspect of murder. Vi wasn't just fighting for her and Jack. The more she realized she might lose those souls—maybe they were dreams, but they felt real. They felt like she was missing beings who she hadn't quite met yet, and she was losing them if she lost their father.

Never, Violet thought. She glanced through the room one more time, standing in front of the door and taking the whole room in. The bed had been turned, and nothing. The drawers had been emptied and strewn. They'd run their hands under every drawer and pulled each out to ensure there was nothing hidden in any way.

Bed, vanity, small table, chairs. A very large wardrobe, so huge Violet didn't think Gertrude could have possibly moved it, but Violet and Clara had done their best to ensure that nothing was hidden behind it all the same.

Violet sighed and turned away and then paused. She turned back, crossing the room to stare at the wardrobe.

"I looked it over twice, Violet," Clara said from near the door. "We really should leave before someone comes back and sees what we've done."

"Mr. Yardley will know the instant it's reported."

"But he'll never *tell*," Clara said. "Someone else might. Father will say that you and Algie have been a bad influence on me. He's looking for reasons to wear me down and make me throw Algie over."

Violet wasn't really listening. She cast Clara a look that ordered her to stand up for herself while she opened the vanity and noted the flat ceiling of the piece. She backed up, looking up at the wardrobe that was taller that Vi. It was an etched and carved antique with shining wood that showed tender care. The carvings came to a peak of curls and whirls made with shining cherry wood.

"Vi!" Clara hissed. "Please! I'll never hear the end of it if we are caught."

Violet ignored Clara, crossed to the vanity, picked up the stool, and set it in front of the wardrobe. She stood up carefully and ran her hand along the top until she felt the leather edges of some sort of bag.

Violet pushed up on her toes and felt around until she found the handle and then took down a beautiful, locked hatbox. Vi didn't wait, she just walked towards the door, opened it, and ordered, "Hurry up now."

Jack's auto had been taken by the valet, and Violet couldn't be seen with her contraband. She hurried to the elevator, rang the bell, and then stepped back so the attendant couldn't see her. Before the doors opened, Violet hissed to Clara, "See if it's Cooper."

"Who?" Clara asked dumbly.

"Cooper!" Violet hissed, tucking her stolen items inside a cabinet that was topped with a vase.

The bell rang and the doors opened. "Hello, Miss. What floor please."

Clara stuttered for a moment and then she asked, "Cooper?"

"Yes, miss."

Vi tucked her face around the side of the elevator and grinned brightly at him. "Cooper, my hero. There's fifty quid in it for you if you get the contents of that cabinet for me to the alleyway outside."

His gaze widened.

"Fifty more if you never speak of it."

"Never," Cooper swore. "I—" He cleared his throat, eyes shining for a moment and then said, "I'll be there. I'd have done it for free."

"I wouldn't have trusted you with it if I didn't already like you," Violet told him, shaking his hand, to Clara's open-mouthed shock.

"Get inside," Violet hissed. "Someone will see you."

Clara hopped onto the elevator, and Violet told Cooper conversationally, "You picked us up in the lobby after we came in from a ramble."

"I sure did, ma'am."

"We looked a bit windblown. Red-cheeked even, as though we'd been walking briskly."

"It's a cool day. A speedy step keeps you warm in the wet London air."

"Indeed," Violet told him, handing him her card. "There's work for you if you ever want it. If all goes well when you come by, I'll be on my honeymoon, but my brother will put you to work until I get back. Victor Carlyle. He'll have heard of you."

Cooper's gaze focused on the card, and he nodded. "You'll be seeing me."

CHAPTER FIFTEEN

*V*iolet collected Jack in the hall outside the suite as he and Algie had already left Roche's rooms. She grinned at Jack, winking happily, and he immediately knew she had done something naughty. He shot her an inquiring look, but Violet wasn't going to answer while they had an audience.

"I'll be by to see Denny soon," Algie promised as Clara put her hand on the crook of his elbow.

"Wonderful," Violet told him brightly. When they returned to the elevator, it was unattended. Violet grinned as Jack selected the floor.

"Odd," he said.

Vi just smirked.

"Hmm," he replied. "You did like him from the moment he chose his brother. That story could have been a lie."

"It wasn't."

"You know that by woman's intuition?"

"Certainly." Violet took advantage of the empty elevator to press up on her toes and kiss Jack on the bottom of his jaw. He was too tall for her to reach much higher, but his fingers dug into her back, and she knew he was no more unaffected than she.

"Do you ever think about the children we'll have some day?"

He paused, looking down at her in surprise, but he didn't hide the truth from her. "I'm looking forward to them, when you're ready."

"They're heavy on my mind," Violet told him.

He rubbed his chin over the top of her head and then pressed a kiss on her forehead. It took a long moment for him to say, "If you want to end things to protect them, Vi, I understand."

She smiled into his chest. It was a sad smile. "I never really thought about children too seriously before you. Don't you see? They won't exist without you, Jack."

"But you could have children without me, Vi."

"Those aren't the children haunting me. Those aren't the ones I'm missing."

"Missing? As though they were on a long journey?"

Vi nodded. She didn't care if it seemed silly. Jack could handle her silliness and everything else she was.

"I—" He didn't say anything else, and she didn't mind. It felt almost as though he were trying on the idea of those children for size. Maybe he was, maybe he wasn't, but she'd tried on the idea of them for size and found that there was an empty place in her heart that was already being filled by them.

"I adore you, Violet Carlyle," he said. "The day you're Violet Wake-field will forever be my favorite moment."

The elevator door opened and Violet stepped out of his arms, ignoring the shocked look on the faces of the elderly couple waiting to get on.

"Cheeky," the woman hissed.

Vi winked in reply.

"What did you find out?" Violet asked as she tucked her hand into Jack's and followed him to the valet, who went running for Jack's auto. Mr. Yardley saw Vi and nodded once before he said, "I believe your friend has already made her way to your auto."

"One of your staff helped me out with a little matter," Violet told him. "Cooper's a good man."

Yardley nodded while Jack gave Violet a sharp glance. She walked with him to the area where the auto would be brought and glanced to the right. Cooper was waiting with a box in his hands.

Vi nodded once and when Jack's auto was brought to the hotel, Violet stepped back as Jack opened the door. She nodded at Cooper, who walked casually over, opened the back door and placed the box inside the auto.

"Ma'am," he said.

Violet handed him a note for her man of business along with the usual tip. He grinned at her. "Your offer couldn't have come at a better time, ma'am. I'd like to be noble and tell you to keep it, but—"

"Vi?" Jack asked, but Violet just waved him off.

"I'll be offended if you don't take me up on for what you did," she said to Cooper. "I know the risk you took, and I won't have it be unrewarded—not even for your very respectable honor."

Cooper searched her face before nodding at Jack. The elevator attendant said, "You're a lucky man, sir." Then he shut the door to the auto before either of them could reply.

"He's not wrong," Violet told Jack.

"I'm aware," Jack said.

He focused on entering the busy traffic while Violet leaned back, exhausted. The dynamics of the Roche family were almost as melodramatic as the dynamics of her own family.

"We should set some private detectives on the Roche crew."

"With special emphasis on Barty and Gertrude," Violet agreed. "Those two are—well..." She shrugged as she glanced at Jack, wickedly grinning. "I like them better than Father Roche but not by very much."

"Agreed. Leaving me alone with him and Algie made me actually sympathetic for poor Algie. A lifetime of that—"

"Won't happen," Violet interrupted. "Clara has decided Roche is going back to the United States and she's staying here with Algie. She won't subject her love to her father."

Jack choked on a surprised laugh. "I'll never cease being surprised by you wonderful creatures."

She changed the subject to the traffic and then the weather, and then they were back to Victor's house. Violet hesitated when she saw the uniformed policeman outside of the house.

"Never fear, Vi." Jack opened the door for her as one of the servants ran down to drive the auto to the garage. Violet glanced at servant and then whispered to him, "Smuggle the contents of that box into the house, please."

"There's one in the kitchens, my lady," he said, directing his gaze to the local policeman.

"Is there now," Violet sighed. She glanced at Jack, who said, "Drive to the salon Violet likes. You know the one?"

The servant nodded.

"There are some items on hold there for her. Have those boxed up with the contents of Violet's box. Tell the girls to make sure the most embarrassing pieces are on the top and to add more if they need to. Whatever it takes to thoroughly hide what Violet has."

The servant nodded while Jack held out his hand for Violet. They walked up the steps as though they weren't being watched by the constabulary, as the servant drove the auto around the side of the house, no doubt meaning to use the delivery drive to escape on his errand.

"Do you think that they know about what we're up to?" Vi asked.

"Nothing we're doing is criminal, Vi," Jack said. "Don't worry."

She cleared her throat, trying for an innocent expression. It didn't work. "I—"

"Tell me nothing," Jack ordered. "I won't lie to the detective."

"Then you need to avoid the parlor," Violet told him.

The constable eyed Violet and Jack but said nothing. Jack opened the door and walked into the entrance hall where Hargreaves was standing at the ready. He was not blocking the parlor door while very carefully blocking the parlor door.

"Why are the constables here when the murder happened two doors down?" Violet demanded.

A voice from Victor's office answered her. "I fear some of the main suspects are in this house, ma'am."

Violet met the gaze of the detective that Ham had assigned to this case. He was so ethical that no one who worked at Scotland Yard would doubt if he suggested Jack wasn't the criminal, and he'd turned his attention Jack's way. Violet's nails dug into Jack's arm even as she smiled at the detective.

"Are you stupid?" she asked merrily.

"I would like to talk to Mr. Wakefield. It's necessary to do my work thoroughly and well, my lady."

"Then I suggest you find the killer."

"I realize you may have meddled in these types of investigations before, my lady. Surely, you've noticed that—"

"Enough," Jack snapped. "Violet is going to defend me until her dying breath, Clarkson. I have been expecting you and I'll do whatever I can to help you get a handle on the information you need. I trust you to do your job."

The detective paused. He seemed a little relieved and Violet might have felt a flash of sympathy if the suspect were any other man. Investigating your superior's best friend had to be the worst assignment you could be given. "Mr. Carlyle said I could use his office while I was here. If you wouldn't mind?"

The detective stepped back and gestured for Jack, who nodded and entered the room as though he were the guest.

"Send in sandwiches and coffee to them," Violet told Hargreaves. "We've had a trying morning, and it's been far too long since breakfast. I'm sure they can both use a little sustenance."

"Yes, ma'am." He didn't move, and Violet realized that he was guarding the door to the parlor. She smiled at him, perhaps a little shiny-eyed for either of their comfort, but he opened the door for her, blocking the entrance with his body after she slipped past.

When she glanced around the room, she found that the chalk-boards had been completely redrawn and the names had gone from a huge number—nearly unattainable—to far fewer.

"What are we left with?"

"Seven," Lila said. She was lying on the Chesterfield with her arm over her eyes. "We were down to four, but we've had to add three more from that John Smith fellow. He might have a pretty face"— Lila lifted her arm from her eyes and glanced at Vi—"but he's terrifying. I'll have one of your nightmares about him ferreting out my secrets."

Denny groaned. "Vi, there's some of those chocolate cocktails and sandwiches. Lila, darling one, you have no secrets."

Lila had dropped her arm back over her eyes and she groaned, sounding like a softer echo of Denny. "That does make me feel better. Everyone already knows my flaws."

Violet stared at them, kicked off her shoes, dropped her coat and then demanded, "Did you see the detective?"

"We pretended we weren't here," Lila said. "Victor didn't give them the freedom of the house. He let one back to talk to the servants since they're all emphatically loyal and he let the detective into his office."

"All he's going to find in there, should he snoop, is novels abandoned before we finished them."

Violet skimmed the names on the boards. They were, each of them, circled. She felt very little surprise to read:

Robert Roche

Robbie Roche

Barty Roche

Gertrude Campbell

Lyle Longfellow

Henrietta Moore

The last name, however, shocked Violet. It was Emily Allen. Vi gasped. "I saw her there. She didn't leave."

"She also says she was in the ladies, but Gertrude didn't mention her and Miss Allen didn't mention Gertrude."

Violet rubbed her hand along her collarbone then fiddled with her engagement ring. Emily Allen had made it known that she wanted another chance with Jack. Would she have framed him for murder if she realized it would never happen? One of those pulp novel plot points where the villain says, if I can't have her, no one can?

Violet couldn't quite see it.

"Why Miss Allen?"

Denny hopped up from his relaxed position, poured Violet a cocktail and pressed it into her hand. He was grinning and bouncing on his toes. "She was a sometime lover of Theo," Denny said almost gleefully. "How absolutely fabulous would it be if she were the killer."

"Miss Allen!" Vi gasped. She winced in sympathy for the woman. She'd had Jack's heart and thrown it away to fall to the likes of Theo.

"Can you imagine?" Lila asked dryly, without lifting her arm.

"I would prefer not to," Vi answered, sipping the cocktail that it was far too early into the day to drink. She sighed. "Just because she was his lover? How did he get someone as clever as Miss Allen?"

"I'll never understand females," Denny declared. "Even I knew Theo was an abrasive misogynist, and I'm a man. Yet the bloke had a whole slew of females. Some duke's daughter, an American, a Russian, two French women, along with Miss Allen."

"He wasn't terrible to look at," Lila said, finally sitting up. She glanced at Violet. "I've never worked harder. This is your birthday present and your Christmas present. We worked Kate into a headache and a nap. Victor went off with the pretty private detective, and the bulk of this was left to poor Denny and me."

"What else did the pretty detective find out?"

"Theo was arrogant." Denny sipped his cocktail while Violet shot him an irritated glance. They *knew* that already.

"What he means," Lila said, taking her husband's cocktail to sip for herself, "is that Theo kept a ledger and didn't bother to use code or anything. You told the diabolical one to strip Theo bare, and it turns out all he had to do was pick a lock and read through Theo's papers. Now he's off trying to rule out which of Theo's marks couldn't have killed him."

Violet closed her eyes in relief. She would fall to her knees later and have a prayer of gratitude for that break. She wasn't sure that anything could help them more.

"So Gertrude doesn't have an alibi? I stole a hidden locked bag from her room, but we're smuggling it in with apparently a gift full of embarrassing things from the salon in case the police decide to search incoming packages."

Lila gasped. "Jack bought you lingerie! I knew he was struggling harder than it seemed to keep to his chaste resolutions."

"Lila, my pet," Denny said, "Anyone with eyes could tell that. Poor Violet's had the breath kissed from her in every corner of this house. My own eyes have been burned more than once."

Violet ignored their banter and stared at the names. Perhaps with the information she'd gotten from Hotel Saffron, they'd be able to rule out or confirm one of the Roche party. They were the most obvious ones. She crossed to the line of chalkboards surrounding the room and erased one that had been thoroughly crossed out.

"Where's Beatrice?" Vi asked absently.

"Collating all of our data on the remaining names. Re-reading to see if she can find any holes, and typing it all up for Ham."

Vi nodded as she stared at the blank door. Her mouth twisted as she considered where to start. A moment later the door to the parlor opened and Jack walked in, closing it behind him. His jaw was tight, and his eyes were blank when Violet looked his way.

She shook her head and he simply crossed to her, taking her hand and jerking her into his arms. She was trembling, tears burning as she whispered, "No, no, no, no."

"It's just for a more thorough questioning."

"Why?" Violet demanded. "Why?"

"It was my knife that killed Theo," Jack said. "I just identified it."

"Why didn't you lie?" she hissed at him.

"It has a rather telltale sign on it that it's mine, Vi. Ham already knew. They'd checked it for prints and mine were on it, Vi. Happily, whoever used it smudged my prints with their grasp using a handkerchief or gloves or something. Ham knew it was mine the moment he saw it. He's concentrating on the fact that I didn't wipe my prints but someone hid theirs."

"Where is he? How could he! Why didn't *he* lie?"

Jack pulled back and kissed her hard before he spoke. "*Trust* Ham!"

She couldn't hold back the tears, but she was trying. She didn't want Jack to be arrested with the memory of her crying in the parlor.

"Where was it, old man?" Denny asked.

"In my desk," Jack sighed. "Easily found if you wanted to find it. I used it to open letters and to remind me of those days."

"Why?" Violet demanded. "Why didn't you have a dull letter opener like everyone else?"

"Because when we remember our dark days," Jack said against her forehead, "we appreciate our lighter days. I kept it as a reminder of the things that have changed. You're the star in my skies, Vi. My sun. The lantern on the hill. You're all of it—that bedamned knife was my reminder of the darker days."

Violet bit down on her bottom lip to keep from crying and wrapped herself tightly around him. She didn't know how long it took for Hargreaves to enter silently and cross to Jack, speaking low, because she was focusing on the sound of his heartbeat and the scent of him.

"It will be fine," Jack told her as he kissed her once more. "Ham has a plan."

"You're lying to me," she told him, holding back the wail that they were supposed to be married in less than twenty-four hours.

He grinned for a moment, that penetrating gaze moving over her as if he were memorizing her and he winked. "Only a little."

CHAPTER SIXTEEN

*V*iolet stared at the parlor door Jack just closed. She could feel the gazes of Denny and Lila, and it made it all the worse. She didn't speak as she walked to the same door, opened it, and stepped into the entrance hall. It was already empty, and Violet took a broken, halting breath before she ran up the stairs to her bedroom. Her spaniel, Rouge, was waiting as though she'd known Violet might need her. Violet let them both in, closing the door behind her and leaning against it.

As if Rouge somehow knew Violet was lost inside of her mind, the sweet little dog put a paw on Violet's foot to anchor her from her thoughts. Vi stared down at the little dog and slowly slid to the floor, pulling her knees against her chest. Stabbed, with Jack's knife, after Jack dragged Theo into the garden, and Jack was found standing over the body. She'd have laughed at the sheer cruelty of it if she'd been capable of making a noise at all. Instead, she put her chin on her knees and stared at the floor of her bedroom.

Violet wasn't sure how much time passed while she sat against her bedroom door. She was beyond being able to write out her feelings in her journal, beyond being able to think anything at all. If her body could have turned off breathing, it would have. There was an abyss inside of her, one Violet didn't dare think about or approach. She hoped if she waited long enough she'd be able to think well enough to come up with a plan.

There was a knock on her door sometime later. Vi could tell that time had passed because her bottom was numb and her back hurt, but it had seemed like only moments.

"Violet," the hushed voice called. "Vi, darling. Please open up."

Vi sort of grunted. She wasn't ready yet. If she'd have cried, perhaps she could have faced someone else, but she hadn't cried yet. She felt like a dam about to burst. She traced her fingertips over the swirls of wood on the floor. What was she going to do? Her wedding was supposed to be the next day.

Had the detective waited until the last minute before the wedding so Jack didn't flee? Violet felt certain that the clever detective might have done just that. Or perhaps, Violet thought, the detective had given them as long as possible to solve the case and they'd failed.

"Violet," the voice said a little sharper, "darling, if you don't open the door, I fear we'll have to force the issue."

Violet blinked as she heard her name called again. There was the quiet murmur of conversation, and Violet slowly realized they meant for her to open the door *or else*. She pushed herself to her feet and, like an automaton, opened the door and stared at the faces on the other side.

Kate, of course, that was who had been speaking. Vi's sister, Isolde, was there, her wide, blue eyes making Violet feel as though she should be more capable. Vi always felt as though she were supposed to be strong around Isolde, but not this time. Even Denny and Lila had wide, panicked gazes.

That would have been enough, but there were servants there as well. Beatrice, Violet's steady maid and assistant. Even the butler, Hargreaves, was present, and he didn't have his expressionless face on.

"Violet," Kate said. "Oh darling, haven't you cried at all?"

Violet shrugged and tucked her hair behind her ear.

"Victor hasn't come back yet," Kate said, eyes welling with tears.

"I'm afraid I don't know what to do." The tears slipped over Kate's face, but Violet turned away. "We've sent servants and Tomas everywhere we could think of to locate Victor, but he's working with Mr. Smith on the investigation."

Beatrice cleared her throat as Violet only nodded. After a moment, Violet spoke, since they seemed to be waiting for her to do so. "All right then."

"What do you want us to do?" Kate asked, still crying. Her tears were silent things, rolling down her cheeks.

"Is the servant back with the things I took from the Roches?"

They all shook their heads.

"Then nothing, I suppose," Violet said, turning to go back to her room. Maybe this time she'd stare at the floor from a chair.

Lila grabbed Violet's arm and snapped, "No!"

"No?" Violet blinked rather stupidly.

Lila yanked her into the hallway with a strength Violet wasn't aware Lila possessed. Vi's best friend dragged her down to the gymnasium and shoved Violet in front of the punching bag as everyone followed. Violet glanced at Lila and then beyond to the whole circle of friends and family.

"Punch it," Lila ordered.

"Why?"

"If you won't cry, you have to get it out another way."

"It?" Violet pressed her hand against her forehead. Maybe she had gone mad. Maybe Jack wasn't being questioned at Scotland Yard for a crime he didn't commit, maybe she was just having a very terrible, very real-feeling dream.

"Whatever you're boxing up inside of that heart of yours would leave me curled up on a sofa screaming to the heavens."

Violet stared at the punching bag, knowing she hadn't gone mad and that this *was* really happening. She slowly curled her hands into a fist and punched it into the bag.

"Please," Lila said sarcastically. "Lady Eleanor could hit harder than that."

Violet hit the punching bag again.

"She'd laugh at you for that," Lila told Violet. "Then she'd get one of her *real* children to do it better."

Violet scowled fiercely as Isolde gasped. "Lila!"

Vi hit the punching bag harder the next time, and she felt the sting in her hands. That felt right. How she should feel, if she could feel.

"Again," Lila ordered.

Violet hit it again, and she didn't need another order to keeping going. She kept hitting it. Behind her there was whispered conversation, but Violet wasn't listening. She focused on the sound of her breathing, the sound of the blood in her ears, the sound of her hands slamming into the punching bag. Maybe if she hit the bag hard enough she'd be struck by some inspiration that told her what to do next.

"Beatrice," Violet snapped as she paused after a particularly hard strike. "Did you find anything out while you were compiling? Anything that was missed before?"

Beatrice gasped at the sudden question and then shook her head. Violet looked back to the punching bag. If Jack were here and this case were a little less personal, what would Violet be doing? She started punching again even though her hands had begun to pulsate with each beat of her heart. She didn't stop even though her ring was digging into her finger. She didn't stop even though an occasional tear slipped down her cheek, even though she was being watched like a mouse surrounded by hawks, even though what she was doing felt useless and worthless.

Finally, Denny lifted her physically and pulled her away. "Vi, darling, that's enough. Generally we wrap our hands or wear gloves. Your fingers are going to be bruised and sore."

Violet stared at him. "I don't know what to do."

"Let's do what we always do," Denny suggested. "Lila, Kate, and I —we've been working on it. We narrowed things down for you, Vi," Denny said. "Let's go stare at the chalkboards, find the fiend, and get Jack back."

Violet couldn't stop the stray tear or two, and she bit down on her lip to keep even more from coming. Denny tucked Violet's hurting hand under his elbow and drew her from the gymnasium. He chattered about Jack as they went. About how poor Detective Clarkson wasn't ready for someone as clever as Jack.

"He should have lied to the detective, made them work for it," Violet told Denny, furious all at once.

"I'd have," Denny agreed. "I'm generally useless, but I can be counted on to look after myself."

"He's too busy focusing on—on—ah!"

"What's right and moral?" Denny asked with a little smile. "He does seem to be one of those rare birds who worries about such things. It might be one of the things you love about him."

"Do you remember when he came back from that case with the orphans on his mind? The children whose father had killed the mother?"

Denny nodded. "Who can forget? We had little ones in the house."

"Jack doing the right thing and being honorable is why they're Kate's adopted siblings now."

Denny nodded. "It's a compromise, really. When you go for the good man, you get the good with the good."

"What does that even mean, laddie?" Lila demanded.

"It means," Denny said as if it were obvious, "that you get the good deeds like finding homes for the orphans and the good deeds like being honest to the constabulary."

Vi groaned. "I do love that I can trust him. Damn it!"

"It's why we're so great," Denny told Violet. "You and me, Vi. We'll do the—ah—more questionable things for him. We'll figure out who the killer is. We'll track them down like a dog in the nighttime, and we'll tell lies to trap them if we have to. Pretend we witnessed what they did. Whatever it takes. Torture even."

Violet nodded and walked into the room. "We have all this transcribed?"

Beatrice nodded. "I kept notes the whole way through, my lady. I have every layer of it written down and much of that typed up, but I did start with what seemed most relevant."

"Clean the boards," Violet told Beatrice. "Please."

"Hargreaves," Isolde said, "go and get Violet some sandwiches or something. She won't be able to be the witty, clever version of herself if she doesn't fuel her brain."

"I'm not hungry," Violet told Isolde.

"I'm not taking no for an answer," Isolde told Violet. "You'll eat if I have to sit on you and force feed you."

"Why aren't you sicking up into a pot and bemoaning the idiocy that led you to create life? Why aren't you terrified of Father finding out that after threatening your beloved, he still took you to bed before you were wed?"

"Vi," Denny groaned. "Don't rhyme. It makes me laugh and then I feel like a right wart."

Isolde just lifted a brow and crossed her arms over her chest. "Did you want to see if you can win a wrestling match against me? I'm quite a bit larger than you. You'll eat," she threatened, "or I'll force feed you."

"She's been training in jiu jitsu, and she's meaner," Denny told Isolde. "You'll definitely lose, dear one. But please, duel it out, and I'll be happy to take notes."

"Enough," Violet said, taking the chalk from Beatrice as the woman wheeled a clean chalkboard to the center of the working space. "I'll eat if you'll leave me be."

Slowly, Violet drew a grid on the chalkboard with a list of names down the side and a list of motives across the top. The names read:

ROBERT ROCHE
ROBBIE ROCHE
BARTY ROCHE
GERTRUDE CAMPBELL
LYLE LONGFELLOW
HENRIETTA MOORE
EMILY ALLEN

Violet glanced at Beatrice. "Repeat these names on that board with what you've learned about each of them so far."

While Beatrice started working on the next chalkboard, Violet wrote the list of motives.

GREED
LOVE

JEALOUSY
HATRED
MERCY
SELF DEFENSE
ANGER
POWER

As Beatrice cleaned and then wrote down notes about each of the suspects, Violet flipped through the pages of notes that Beatrice was condensing. Vi didn't want to miss any details, even though when Beatrice was done, Violet felt as though her new assistant had done a good job of pulling out the most telling details.

The sandwiches arrived and Isolde made a plate for Vi while she read through the transcribed notes. There were details Violet would never have suspected, things like where and how Robert Roche made his money along with Barty's favorite gambling establishments.

Violet was shocked her private investigators had found this much out so quickly. She had hardly been present while they'd been bringing in reports. Violet read while Isolde forced Vi through two cups of coffee and a full sandwich, and Lila and Kate went to take yet another report in one of the smaller parlors.

"Are the local bobbies still here?"

Denny sniffed, glancing at Vi before he answered. "The one in the kitchens is still interviewing servants and taking notes about whatever nonsense he deems interesting. The one on the front steps left when they took Jack in, but I think we're being watched across the way."

Violet crossed to the window and lifted a brow when she saw a fellow sitting in an auto. He wasn't even trying to hide. The servant who had taken Jack's auto to the garage was walking down the street with a rather large box in his hands. He entered the gate and went around to the back entrance while Violet paused.

The bloke in the auto noted the servant, even writing something down in a notebook, but he didn't get out of the auto or approach the servant.

"Beatrice, go get the package from Lenny. He just came back from picking it up. Make a big deal about it being unmentionables for my honeymoon and make sure the bobby doesn't get too many answers."

The woman nodded and hurried out of the room while Violet stared again at the chalkboards. Her mind was still scattered, but it was in better shape than her heart. She felt as though that thing that should be keeping her alive had abandoned its duty to curl up in the corner of her soul. Any moment now, she'd drop and Jack would be left to his fate—whatever that might be.

CHAPTER SEVENTEEN

*V*iolet had crossed back to the chalkboard. She looked up to see Ham come in. She shot him a withering glare, but he didn't wince. He watched her as though he were protecting her *for* Jack. Violet had little doubt that Ham would probably return to Jack that night and report on her state of being. She ignored Ham for the moment. She knew Jack's presence at Scotland Yard wasn't Ham's fault, but she very much wanted to blame him. Rather than destroying their friendship, she screwed her mouth shut and turned back to the notes she was reading.

Eventually she looked up again and found Rita sitting next to Ham, whispering to him. There was a box in the corner of the room where Beatrice was reading through the things Violet had stolen from the hotel with Rita and Ham helping. Vi hadn't noticed their arrival but she was happy to see Rita there. No doubt she could convey all she'd learned from the hotel to Beatrice while Violet attempted to think.

Violet paced, staring at the three names and Beatrice's notes.

BARTY ROCHE—not in Mr. Robert Roche's will. Barty had already lost one fortune and was living off the charity of relatives who let him pretend to a level of income he no longer could claim. He wasn't entirely without funds as he still owned half the company Mr. Roche still ran, but the company had taken a turn for the worse and the income wasn't enough to pay Barty's gambling debts.

Barty was seen leaving the hotel often and was usually going to gamble or clubs with gamblers that often ended in private card games with high stakes. He's certainly in rather a lot of debt.

Violet looked up from her pacing and called, "Does Barty keep records of his debts?" Had Violet stolen those when she took his papers?

"These are mostly letters from his daughter. There's scraps of what must be copies of IOUs or notes to himself, but he's as careless with those as he is with his daughter." Beatrice disgust warmed Violet's heart.

"There are, however," Ham stated, "check stubs for rather extravagant amounts from Robbie Roche's account. They're all written to Theodophilus Smythe-Hill."

"Robbie?" Violet's mouth dropped, then she wondered aloud. "What brought about that generosity?"

"I wonder if Robbie found it worth killing over," Ham added. "If he realized—"

"Did anyone send for Clara and Algie?" Violet asked, tired of asking questions they couldn't answer. "Did they charge Jack?"

Ham shook his head and said low, "It's not looking good right now, Vi. But we aren't done trying yet."

Violet didn't want to think about that. She needed the answer, but she turned back to the chalkboard with a roiling stomach as she faced the notes about Robert Roche.

ROBERT ROCHE raised Barty Roche and watched his nephew reach his majority and throw away the entire fortune that his father and uncle had created for him. He refuses to pay Barty any money, but he was actively working to help Barty marry Gertrude Campbell, even telling the lie that they were in love.

Mr. Roche was the one who invited Theo to the party, but any of his party might have known of his actions. He was the one who tried to get Violet and Jack involved.

Violet sighed as she read. It was all damning but without a shred of evidence to believe that Mr. Roche had been the one who followed Jack and Theo to the garden and waited until Jack had walked away with his cigar.

"Bloody hell!" Violet hissed. "The cigar."

"The cigar?" Ham asked suddenly.

"How could they know that Jack wouldn't come back in right away? *You* might have known he'd walk off his anger with a cigar and some cooler air, but who else could know that except Miss Allen?"

"Does that mean she's our main suspect? Please say she is," Denny crowed, a little too happily for Violet's taste.

She shook her head, remembering all too well another scene.

"Don't you see? The first party, at Hotel Saffron, Jack dragged Theo out and had a cigar before he returned to the ballroom, having to hunt us down in the suite. Everyone in that suite would know that including all of the Roche party."

"Then," Ham added, "one of them made sure Theo would be at the second party. How quickly did you invite Algie?"

"The moment we decided to have it," Violet said. "A cousin we like —he was on the list right below all of you."

"So," Kate said, taking in a breath, "one of them decided to use the chance to get rid of Theo. We need Clara. We need to know if the invite to Theo was from her father or if he was manipulated to do it."

Violet stared at the last name.

GERTRUDE CAMPBELL. She didn't have nearly as much to lose. A fiancé who had already lost a fortune. To anyone else's account, she'd come out ahead if Barty had to be left behind.

Violet turned back to pacing between the chalkboard and the room. With enough time maybe she'd be struck by lightning and shocked into a revelation. Seven private investigators, Ham directing the case at Scotland Yard, an earl, Jack's powerful father, *all* of their friends, and still her fiancé wasn't going to make it to their wedding.

CHAPTER EIGHTEEN

*V*iolet was still staring at her blank board while Beatrice finished transcribing her notes. Violet glanced at what Beatrice had done, but she was back to feeling scattered again. Victor arrived as Violet finally stood and crossed out the section that transected the motive self-defense and each of the killer names.

If there was a thing that Theo's murder was *not,* it was self-defense. A knife in the back? Violet thought back and then asked, "There were no signs of a struggle, am I right?"

"You're right," Victor answered. Violet spun and their gazes met. She knew immediately he'd received the news of Jack's location. "He wasn't killed out of mercy either."

There was so much going unsaid between the twins that it seemed they were speaking more with their eyes and their expression than would have ever been possible with their words.

Vi waited, staring at her brother, seeing his heart breaking for her, his worry, his dreadful concern at her wooden state. She was barely functioning, and she was too well aware of it, but he might be *even* more aware of it.

"I was with Algie and the Roches at the club," Victor said, "when I got word. They didn't hear, but they will. I abandoned them and found Father."

"Father?" Vi asked in surprise. She hadn't even considered what her father might have been able to do.

Victor squeezed her hand, carefully not hugging her so she wouldn't fall apart. "He went down with a whole gaggle of powerful men. If it is possible to avoid charging Jack with a crime, they will. If they can't, they'll delay as long as possible."

Violet nodded, her mouth dry.

Victor looked beyond Violet to the chalkboard. "How long has she been staring at it?"

"Too long," Denny answered. "I'm tempted to fill it in myself."

Violet shot Denny a nasty glance and he held up surrendering hands. "I know I wouldn't be as helpful as you, Vi. I just want to help."

Violet's gaze teared up at that and Denny winced. "Please don't."

She tried for a smile and failed, but at least the tears dried up.

"Thank god," Denny muttered as Violet rubbed her hand over her face.

"The wedding is supposed to be tomorrow," Violet said. "We won't make it."

They were all silent staring at her. Probably imagining what she was feeling. She wasn't feeling much—would any of them guess that? That her mind and heart had shut down.

Finally Isolde said, "There are other days."

Kate nodded, crying for Violet once again as she added, "You won't care what day it is when you get married."

Violet nodded, smiling one of those lying smiles. "If we don't get to go on our honeymoon, do you think Jack will tell me where we would have gone?"

Victor pressed a hand against his chest as if he felt what she was supposed to be feeling and then glanced at the board again.

"Jealousy is a good motive for Miss Allen. She does hate you."

Violet followed his gaze and then walked over to the board, marking that spot with a large X, taking the chance to put slashes through the mercy box for every name on the list. It was hardly merciful to murder some man in the garden and frame Violet's betrothed.

"She might not have killed for money," Lila added, sniffing away a sympathetic tear. "But love, hatred, and anger all fit for her."

Violet woodenly placed large X's in each of those boxes for Miss Allen, putting a solitary slash through each of the remaining options.

She glanced at Mr. Roche and then placed X-marks in the hatred, anger, and power boxes with slashes through each of the remaining boxes.

Then in a fury of emotion, Violet crossed out the entire rows of Henrietta Moore and Lyle Longfellow. Maybe they had killed Theo, but Violet didn't think they'd prove such a thing before her wedding. She'd throw those names to Scotland Yard or the private detectives. There was little chance she'd be able to do anything about them regardless.

She focused on the next name. Robbie Roche was, she thought, the least likely Roche to kill Theo unless Theo knew something specific about Robbie that no one else was aware of. Violet didn't bother focusing on him. Instead, she also crossed him out entirely. If something came up, she'd put him back on the list.

That left Violet with Barty Roche and Gertrude Campbell. Violet focused on Barty first. She could see someone like him knifing a man in the back far easier than she could see Gertrude. The spoiled American heiress who should have chosen better versus the man who actually had something to lose.

For Barty, Violet put X-marks in the greed, hatred, anger, and power boxes. She put question marks behind the love and jealousy boxes. Violet suspected that the only thing Barty loved about Gertrude was the size of her inheritance, but they were engaged. Perhaps it wasn't just about the money.

Violet scoffed at the idea and then stared at Gertrude's name. Greed? No. Love? Maybe. Jealousy? Of Theo? No. Of what he knew about Barty? Possibly. Violet left that box blank. Hatred, anger, power, all of those were possible if Gertrude knew that Theo was attempting to blackmail Barty and risking the ruin of her marriage.

"Why didn't she just throw him over?" Violet asked. "She doesn't strike me as dim."

"What do you mean?" Lila asked.

"She has to know he isn't really a teetotaler. She has to know they don't have all that much in common in those moral areas. She isn't getting anything out of it but marriage, and it's not like Barty Roche, the gambler who can't stop betting, isn't irreplaceable. There's no love lost between them. We need Clara," Violet finished.

Vi heard her friends as they talked among themselves while she circled three names. Robert Roche, Barty Roche, and Gertrude Roche. After a moment, Vi added Emily Allen. They were the only possibilities that Violet could follow through the thought line and see it happening that way.

Emily Allen might have killed Theo if he was threatening her. If there was a motive beyond Jack, as much as Violet would like to demonize the woman, she didn't think that Miss Allen would have murdered Theo *just* to torment Jack.

"I'll be wanting Miss Allen as well."

She knew that some of them left, but Violet paid little attention to anything beyond the chalkboards in front of her and the report that Beatrice had made.

She moved to another chalkboard and cleaned it while everyone walked on ice around her. They'd discovered that Theo had paid more than half his bills with income that came from blackmail. He blackmailed everyone he could, from a professor at his college to one of his cousins who probably paid him with pin money.

He really had been a snake. Violet wouldn't have been surprised if he forced himself on some girl and then blackmailed her to keep quiet about it. She gritted her teeth, wishing it had been her hand that had wielded the knife.

"He really did deserve to be removed from existence." Violet flipped back to the early pages about him.

"He wasn't so bad," a familiar voice said, and Violet glanced up to meet the very beautiful gaze of a very beautiful woman.

"He blackmailed his own family, Miss Allen. Doesn't that offend your sense of honor?"

"I've met that cousin," Miss Allen replied. "She is rather awful."

"So she deserved to pay an even more awful person for that?"

Miss Allen glanced her over, and Violet felt as though her protective layers had been stripped away.

"I'm not here to help you," Miss Allen stated flatly, "but I'll do what I can to help Jack."

"Why?"

"Despite his sudden inexplicable attraction to incurable naiveté embodied by you, I loved him once."

Violet found the very claim to be offensive, but she wasn't going to argue with anything that might help Jack. At that moment, she'd have taken it from the devil himself.

"You said in your statement that you were in the ladies just after Jack took Theo out."

"I found the episode rather...disturbing. He was much more controlled when I knew him, not that—that beast. Seeing that he'd descended to a more animalistic version was personally offensive to me."

Violet stared for a moment, trying not to react. Denny started to say something sardonic, but Violet held up her hand. They were *not* going to fight with Miss Allen and waste their energy on her.

"Did you see Gertrude Campbell in the ladies?"

"I was quite alone," Miss Allen replied. "I believe you'll see that in my statement. I can assure you I do not lie to constables."

"Miss Campbell also stated she'd gone there."

"I suppose then," Miss Allen said smoothly, "that you'll have to choose who you believe. However, consider this—I *wasn't* being blackmailed by Theo, and I don't have a reason to have murdered him."

"What about his string of lovers?" Lila asked lazily. "No woman wants to be thrown over for an international checklist of loose women."

Miss Allen turned that way and smiled mockingly. "If I'd wanted a full-time lover, I'd have chosen one. Theo is an excellent dancer, he knows everyone, he can be charming when he chooses, and he no more wanted me long-term than I wanted him. He was, in those respects, a rather perfect lover."

Violet shook her head, trying to decide whether she believed Miss Allen. It didn't, Violet realized, really matter. What she needed was whatever information Miss Allen might have. The horrid woman could possibly shed some light on what happened. Even lies would provide an interesting angle.

"You'd think you'd be more careful about who you suspect with that list of yours." Miss Allen laughed mockingly, gazing at the chalkboards. "Is this really how you do it? You make a game board and gossip and find killers? That can't be right. Jack tells you who the killer is, doesn't he? You've never discovered anything before on your own."

Violet didn't bother sparring with the woman. "Did you know Theo had other lovers?"

"Yes." Miss Allen's mocking smile made Violet want to box her ears.

"Do you know who they were?"

"I didn't care."

Violet sighed.

"You and I both know that the killer is one of the Roche family," Miss Allen said mockingly. "Did Theo blackmail people? Yes. If you found his ledger, you'll see he took a little here and a little there. Not enough to quibble too much over. His side hobby added up to dinners and new suits and extravagances he couldn't normally afford."

"That's true, my lady." Beatrice looked apologetic for agreement. "It seems he was careful to never ask for more than someone could pay. Kate and I guessed he did that to keep them from being too desperate."

Miss Allen smirked before she said, "He was worse with his gambling. He led people into debts that they couldn't afford for his bigger things, but they were still real debts and he wasn't nearly so gentle about his sums."

"Did he cheat?" Denny asked.

"No," Victor sighed. "I looked into it when Algie was caught in Theo's webs. Theo was good at reading people. Especially the blokes we knew from school. He remembered everything. He'd string together the smallest of asides. Since he paid attention to everything and he knew us from our days in short pants, he just discovered things or knew things that anyone else would miss. Then he used them at just the right moment when you were playing a game with him. Few could face that and not falter in their play."

"Perhaps," Violet said, marking the greed box heavier for Barty. "Perhaps he drew Barty in too far and Barty needed an escape that Clara and Algie couldn't pay for."

"If Theo did that," Miss Allen said, "I don't know anything of it, and he tended to be rather chatty with me. What I can tell you is that Gertrude Campbell lied about being in the ladies, and I didn't kill Theo. Believe me if you want to find whoever is framing Jack."

"You were never our strongest suspect anyway," Violet said with a sigh.

"More's the pity," Denny added.

A mere breath later, Lila added, "Hear, hear!"

CHAPTER NINETEEN

*V*iolet looked up when Algie entered soon after Miss Allen left.

"We weren't able to get rid of Gertrude," Algie hissed. "She's clinging like a poisonous spider. Hargreaves seated them in the other parlor. I told Clara and Gertrude I need the toilet to escape."

Victor huffed a laugh while Algie caught Violet's gaze and crossed to her, taking her hands and squeezing them. "No one thinks Jack killed Theo, Vi. You'll come out of this. I'm so sorry your preparations are coming to naught, but you'll still have your happy ever after. I know you will, Vi."

Before Violet could cry, Algie hugged her tightly and then stepped away to shake hands with Victor. The movement gave Violet a chance to trap her emotions and box them into the back of her mind again.

"I'll take care of this Gertrude," Kate said, rising and lifting a brow at Lila. "Come, my girl. We need to give Violet time with Clara, so one of us will have to take Gertrude while the other peels Clara away."

Violet made a timeline on one of the chalkboards as she waited for Clara to arrive, starting with that first party. Because she was a masochist, Violet counted down to day 1. Her timeline read:

DAY 7—Party at the Hotel Saffron, first confrontation with Theo. Jack walks off his anger with a cigar, and everyone sees.

DAY 6—Tea with friends, normal life before all went straight to Hades.

DAY 5— Party to christen the house. Theo is murdered. Jack is framed.

DAY 4—Investigation.

DAY 3— Further investigation—Whoever the killer is, they've hidden behind Jack's broad shadow too well, the bloody devil.

DAY 2—Jack is taken into Scotland Yard.

DAY 1—Wedding day.

Violet frowned at the chalkboard, hating it. It wasn't the delay of her wedding so much as the fear that it would *never* happen. She'd never know the safety of sleeping in Jack's arms again. She'd never meet those children who seemed to haunt her. She'd never grow old next to him and see if he still loved her when she was wrinkled even though she had little doubt they'd have spent the next decades laughing and loving

The chalkboards that were in use were lined side-by-side. There was the one with the seven suspect names that Beatrice had put together. There was the cross-section of motives and suspects. There was Violet's personal list of suspects with only four names, showing both Gertrude and Miss Allen crossed out.

When Clara entered, she joined Violet silently reading the same chalkboards.

"Do you really think that my father or Barty killed Theo?" Clara's voice was breathy, as though she couldn't quite believe it, and Violet realized how hard it must be to see your loved ones' names up there on the suspect list.

No, not realized. She was learning from experience.

Violet shrugged, her ability to empathize severely compromised. Her gaze was still fixated on Day 1. It had been snatched from her now, and she objected strenuously. The next morning she'd wake alone, and when she did, she'd face a room full of people tiptoeing around her because her beloved was accused of murder.

Before she answered, she crossed to the timeline board and wrote out a timeline for the day of Theo's death.

1: People arrive at the new house.

2: Confrontation between Jack and Theo on the floor.

Vi shuddered to think of that. Theo had screamed about Jack's previous love affair with Miss Allen. A love affair that had gone farther than Vi's. Was he just more attracted to Miss Allen? Not, Violet told herself, a problem she needed to give strength to at the moment.

3: Jack drags Theo out of the ballroom and through the French doors to the garden. He throws Theo off the grounds and then walks out his anger with one of those beloved Cuban cigars. (Just as he had at Algie's party.)

"Are you saying," Clara demanded, "that whoever killed Theo was at my party and watched what happened and then engineered it again?"

"That confrontation was particularly delightful," Denny added. "I'd wondered at the time if he'd come to your party, Vi, to say those things specifically. Why come and confront Jack at all? It was like Theo had prepared to hurt you. He had to have known that Jack would win a physical contest. He was willing to risk—"

Vi paused, staring at Denny. "Bloody hell, Denny, you genius." Her hands were shaking as she glanced at Beatrice, who was watching it all carefully.

"Who," Violet demanded, grabbing Clara's arm, "who decided among your family that Theo should be invited?"

Clara's gaze widened and she whispered hoarsely, "Papa."

Algie shook his head. "No, that's not it, love. Robbie did. You had gone to change when Robbie said to your father maybe Jack and Violet would help if Theo was their problem too."

"That never did make sense," Violet snapped. "Why would Jack confronting Theo somehow solve the blackmail problem? I just assumed your father said that because he was angry and wanted to make Jack and me suffer for declining his request for help."

"I—"

"Your father had to know that," Violet added. "He might be abrasive and rude and ready to roll over anyone in his way, but he's not obtuse. This doesn't add up."

"What doesn't?" Denny asked.

Violet crossed to Beatrice's board and erased it as she asked, "What was in the locked case, Beatrice?"

"Letters between Barty and his first wife. They're mostly in Spanish, but Kate translated them."

Violet turned back. "In the locked case?"

Beatrice nodded, glancing down at the stack of papers she'd been reading through. "There's nothing particularly surprising in them. Love letters. Letters about financial issues later. Things about their daughter for a few months before the wife died. Then a few letters between the wife's parents and Barty. They seemed rather fond of him, but they were furious he wasn't doing more to help raise the baby."

"But those were in the *locked* case?"

Beatrice nodded again, staring at Violet as though she'd made a mistake.

"*And* they covered the finances?"

Beatrice's gaze was wide. "It's all there, ma'am. They were struggling to even pay their hotel bill when Mr. Barty left to go ask his uncle for help. Barty had lost all of his funds at that point. His wife died while he was gone. The letters after that are about the money he was supposed to send to help the child. Her parents couldn't afford the baby."

"In the *locked* case?"

"I opened it for her myself, Vi," Ham said, adjusting the case. "Why does it matter?"

"It's Gertrude's case."

Violet turned back to the chalkboard. "It still doesn't add up. Why would Gertrude kill Theo to keep Barty's lies? She was supposedly the only one who didn't know them, yet she knew he lied to her all the time. She knew he left the hotel. She left *after* he did. Even if she didn't follow him, she knew he was out."

"It makes sense," Ham said rising, "if Mr. Roche or Barty killed Theo to keep Barty's secrets *only* if they assumed that Gertrude didn't know them."

"Is it possible that Barty killed to hide a secret that Gertrude already knew and yet still wanted him? Of all the terrible ironies."

"I'm afraid that's not quite accurate," Clara inserted. "Gertrude wouldn't be allowed to marry Barty if his past were to be known because her parents would end it. She *is* an heiress, but she does not have control of her funds."

"I'm confused," Violet said, "by all the secrets and who knew what."

"Make another board," Rita suggested. Vi had nearly forgotten she was there, she'd been so quiet. "Look at it from another angle."

Violet paused and then started:

MR. ROCHE — knew that Barty had lost his fortune and had a child. Knew that Gertrude's fortune was not available if that secret became well-known.

Did not know that Gertrude was aware of Barty's past. Did not know that Gertrude snuck out of the hotel at night.

BARTY ROCHE — knew his own secrets.

Did not know that Gertrude was aware of his past. Did not know that Gertrude snuck out of the hotel at night.

GERTRUDE CAMPBELL — knew that Barty was a liar. Knew that Barty snuck out of the hotel. Snuck out herself. (Where was she going?)

"If she knew," Clara said under her breath, "why did she want him? He's not a devoted lover. He's neglectful."

"When he's around is he attentive?" Violet asked, immediately shaking her head as she remembered the way he treated Gertrude at the first party.

"He's not attentive," Clara said, missing how Violet shook her head. "He's *compliant*. Tells her what she wants to hear and then pats her hand and grins at her as though she's precious. It's not believable when you see how he behaves later, but—"

"Well now," Violet said to Ham. "Compliant is an interesting feature in a man."

"What are Mr. and Mrs. Campbell like?" Ham asked Clara, following Violet's train of thought.

"They're awful," Clara said immediately. "Father, as hard as he is, is a saint in comparison. They control everything. Her dress, her clothes, who she spends time with, even what she eats. She doesn't seem to mind, but I would hate it."

"And suddenly," Violet said, "it all comes clear."

"It does indeed," Ham agreed. "Now to prove it."

"I don't understand," Denny whined. "Explain it for the plebeians."

Ham glanced at the others. "If you scupper this for Jack, I'll ruin you."

"They won't," Victor said. "Algie doesn't want the Roches without the comfort of the Carlyles. And Clara doesn't want a murderer for a cousin-in-law."

"Especially," Violet added, "when she doesn't have custody of the child yet. No one loves the little girl more than Clara."

"You would use the child against me?" Clara asked, her gaze wide and horrified.

"Gertrude would. We won't. Maria needs Gertrude out of Barty's life."

"Explain the murder!" Denny said, stamping his foot. "I don't understand."

Violet wrote out:

DAY 7 - Party at the Hotel Saffron, first confrontation with Theo. Jack walks off his anger with a cigar. Gertrude witnesses it and the fury between Theo and Jack. Perfect for getting rid of her burden.

DAY 5 - Party to christen the house. Somehow Gertrude manipulates things to get Theo invited. Chances are she knew of the black-mail and had—

Violet paused and turned to Clara. "Would Robbie pay blackmail for Barty?"

Clara immediately shook her head

"Would he if he knew that he'd get paid back from Gertrude once she was married?"

Clara's gaze widened. "Perhaps. Almost probably with interest or some other incentive. He's not generous."

Violet returned to Day 5 and wrote: —manipulated or offered Theo something to come and ruin things for Vi and Jack. Theo arrives, delib-erately incites a confrontation with Jack, and is removed from the property. Theo comes back. Why? For another cheque? For something else?

DAY 4- Investigation

DAY 3- Further investigation. Whoever the killer is, they've hidden behind Jack's broad shadow too well.

DAY 2- Jack is taken into Scotland Yard because a knife from his office is used to kill Theo.

Anyone could have guessed there would be some sort of letter opener or object to use for a murder. The knife must have seemed to be god sent.

DAY 1 - Wedding day.

CHAPTER TWENTY

"We need a confession," Ham said. "I can rush things and get Jack out in time for the wedding if we can get a confession."

"How?" Violet asked, rubbing her brow. Her head had been aching for hours, and she was too scared to hope.

"She's here," Denny said. "We lie, we cheat, we...do whatever is necessary. We work together."

"We recruit Miss Allen," Violet said suddenly.

"Em?" Ham asked, flabbergasted.

"Get her back here," Violet said to Victor hurriedly. "Tell her everything. Tell her we need her to lie to Gertrude and tell her that she knows Theo's secrets because she was Theo's lover."

"She'll make you pay," Victor told Violet even as he sent Beatrice running for a servant to get his auto. Perhaps a black cab would be faster?

"We need to ring up Miss Allen," Violet said. "I—"

"I'll do it," Ham said. "She owes me a rather large favor, and I'll be cashing in."

"I'll go with Victor," Rita added. "She'll be nicer if she has an audience connected to her ladies club."

"Thank you," Violet said almost absently. She met Ham's gaze and a swelling of hope filled her. She didn't have the ability to speak while also swallowing the ball of tears that was lodged in her throat, but he seemed to understand.

"Make Gertrude stay," Violet told Clara and Algie. "She's not leaving, but we want her off her guard as well. We need a confession. Bloody hell! We need Ham to hear it, but she won't confess if he's here."

"We could," Beatrice suggested as she came back into the room, "dress the constable in the kitchens in a uniform and have him outside the room with the door open. Even if she sees him, it'll seem like he's just doing his work."

"Ply Gertrude with cocktails, Denny. Those chocolate ones. Tell her they're a special drink you make for Kate's little siblings. You can't really taste the alcohol in them. Let's loosen her tongue."

Denny nodded and crossed to the bar in the parlor, making up the drink with a heavy hand while Violet stared at the chalkboards, hands shaking. This *had* to work. It simply *had to*.

～

"We told her that we had to stay with you," Algie murmured to Violet as they took their seats in the second parlor. "That you were too fragile to leave alone. All hands on deck. Look weak, darling Vi."

Violet nodded. She felt rather weak, and the glimpse she'd caught of herself in the mirror proclaimed just the theme they were looking for. Violet had great canyons under her eyes, only the merest remnants of lipstick on the edges of her lips, and her dress had chalk dust that left her rather grubby.

"Violet," Lila said, handing her a glass of ginger wine. "Here you go, love. Drink up and you'll feel better."

Lila and Kate hadn't had a chance to leave the parlor with Gertrude, so they didn't know what was happening. It seemed that Lila, however, had caught enough of the gist to guess that Gertrude was their target. If Lila had caught on, certainly Kate had as well.

Violet sipped the ginger wine while Denny lied to Gertrude about the contents of the chocolate drink he was offering her. He did it in such a charming way she couldn't really refuse. Hopefully, she didn't just set it aside.

Miss Allen must have been ready when Victor arrived, because they were back before Violet had finished mopping up stray tears. She was getting a lot of, 'You poor dear' and 'Chin up, old girl' from the others. Violet sipped slowly, making every conversation awkward just to watch Gertrude shift.

When Victor arrived with Miss Allen, Gertrude's gaze widened in shock. Rita didn't return, but Violet assumed she was hiding with Ham instead. Violet watched Gertrude while everyone else turned to the new arrivals. Once the initial shock was over, Gertrude's gaze narrowed on Miss Allen.

"I'm sorry," Gertrude said, "I wasn't aware that you were friends."

"Do you know Em?" Violet asked, holding out her hand to Miss Allen as though they were old friends.

"I just...well...I thought that she was once engaged to your Jack, Violet."

Emily laughed merrily. "Children's hijinks. I threw him over when I realized I hadn't seen a bit of the world and wasn't ready to be the old ball and chain."

"Interesting," Gertrude said.

"You know what I think is interesting?" Emily asked brightly. "How you can sit with Jack's beloved and smile so prettily after pinning a murder on him."

Violet blinked in shock that Emily came out with it just like that.

"You're the American that Theo was sleeping with, of course. He told me about his uptight heiress who'd gone wild escaping her parents."

Gertrude blushed.

"Don't worry, darling," Emily said. "The private detectives working for Jack are already tracking down the servants at the hotel where you met Theo. He always sent the same cabbie for you, didn't he? He didn't care about those little details, but they do bite one in the end."

"I'm sure I don't know what you're talking about." Gertrude glanced around, looking for support and finding none.

"I've spoken with their John Smith myself. He's yummy," Miss Allen said. "I told him the names of all the lovers, but Theo called you Trudy, didn't he?"

Oh, Violet thought, oh! Gertrude had gone from red and furious to a little sickly. Violet bit down hard on her abused lip and clenched her bruised fists as Gertrude said, "Even if I was having a liaison, you can't believe that I killed Theo."

"Of course we can," Emily laughed merrily. "We're all ladies here. Trapped by your parents, you found a stooge to marry and get your inheritance. I understand, I do. All of us girls do. We talk about modern times and our freedoms, but we're not really free. Not when someone else holds the purse strings."

"You are speaking lies and nonsense," Gertrude hissed. She started to stand, but Emily rose first and shoved her back down and leaned over her.

"I saw you leave the ballroom. I saw you pretend to walk to the ladies and go into Jack's office. It's not that much farther, is it? I knew you were sleeping with Theo. I wondered if you intended to have an assignation with him. Jack is one of the few men I trust and respect, Miss Campbell. I wasn't going to let you get away with something like that, but you left out the side door. I noticed your arm stiff at your side where you were hiding the knife, but I assumed you were meeting Theo in the gardens. You did, of course. With a knife in your hand and that arrogant fool too certain of himself to realize that a woman could kill him as easily as a man."

"You lie."

"The evidence is stacking against you," Miss Allen said. "You were in the office. Jack would have had to come back inside to get the knife. The jury will hear about how Jack wouldn't have needed to come back for a knife. He's deadly, you know, with just his hands." Miss Allen scrunched her nose and laughed. "They'll hear about how you took a war hero and tried to set him up to cover for your salacious past, and they'll hang you."

"Our cousin ended up in asylum with a good solicitor and a sad story. That won't happen to you," Algie said gently, "if you try to ruin Jack first."

"I'm not confessing." Gertrude laughed but it was an angry, betrayed noise. "You have nothing. Lies from low class servants easily paid to lie. From a whore like Miss Allen. No witnesses. Nothing."

"There's the blood on your dress," Clara said. "I didn't want to believe when I saw it."

Gertrude jumped at that, her gaze fixed on Clara's wide, blue eyes. They were convincing, and Gertrude's fingers twitching at her side conveyed her distress.

"There's the blackmail you were paying," Algie added. "Robbie told me how he was paying for you so he could get more money later. You know how Father Roche watches Robbie so carefully, afraid he's another Barty. Robbie must have jumped at the chance to have money that Father Roche wasn't watching."

"There's no blood," Gertrude hissed. "I had no idea Robbie was paying Theo. Probably to cover for Barty's indiscretions."

"I saw it," Clara said flatly. "I saw it with my own eyes, and you can't hide it once the police take it in. You'll be caught, Gertrude. Confess and ask for mercy."

"The knife was used with a handkerchief," Violet told Gertrude. "Jack's prints were still there, but the killer's were smudged. It will be enough to get Jack off. That mistake alone will free Jack. He'll be free and you'll be taken in, and they'll hang you. I've written a book, you know, about what it feels like to be hanged. I researched it from the few survivors. Strangling is a terrible way to go. Don't think I won't bribe the guard to make sure your neck doesn't break."

Gertrude gasped at Violet's statement, with her hand to her throat.

"Plus," Denny added. "London *loves* Jack. There was an article just yesterday about how he not only found the murderer of a young mother, he ensured her children were adopted into a good home. You're a fool if you don't confess."

"I won't be bullied into confessing," Gertrude hissed. Her gaze was narrowed, and Violet felt a rush of panic. They might get Jack off, but they needed that confession for Violet's wedding to take place the next day.

"Please." Miss Allen laughed again. "Theo told me *everything*."

Gertrude paled. "Why should I believe you? It was your secrets being shouted across the ballroom, not mine."

"Theo said those things because he hated Vi. Who can blame him? Beautiful, rich, never interested in him. He hated her, and he *hated* you. Despised you. Despised your crass American ways. Your clinginess. He'd have thrown you over if you weren't getting him those cheques."

"That's not true," Gertrude said.

"Besides," Miss Allen said, "you aren't as stupid as his normal victims. You knew he'd be coming for you next."

Gertrude said nothing to that.

"Had he already insinuated that you should treat him better? I'll bet that he had. The *key* to having the power over a man like Theo was, of course, to never let him know anything you didn't want the world to know."

"You can't prove that," Gertrude said. "This is all unfair."

"I'll testify myself to how he was with women," Miss Allen said. "I'll make sure the jury knows how trapped you were, so you won't be able to pretend it was a light fling. You were caught like a rabbit in a snare, and they'll know."

"Father had you followed on your liaisons," Clara told Gertrude gently. Clara even reached out and took Gertrude's hand as if she were comforting her. "Oh sweetie, the facts are all there."

"Then why is Jack in Scotland Yard instead of me?" Gertrude hissed triumphantly. "You have *nothing.*"

Well damn it, Violet thought.

Ham walked in then. He glanced around. "Miss Campbell, we need to speak."

"Why?" she hissed. "You have a man in custody."

Ham laughed. "Miss Campbell, we had a cooperative witness who came in to help us clarify a few things. It was the last that we needed to cement the case on you."

"No!" Gertrude said, shoving Miss Allen out of the way. "No, you can't prove I did anything."

"Come, my dear," Ham said. "Witnessed by servants, a history of payments, blood on your dress, no sign of a struggle around the body. It seems like you have everything perfect in the moment."

"There's no evidence that it was me."

"There's rather a *heap of evidence* that it was you. There's no evidence that it was Jack. A few witness statements that Jack had removed Theo from Violet's presence more than once and never did more than rough him up a bit. Jack has an honorable career both in Scotland Yard and in the military. A knife that *didn't* have his prints removed, no sign of a struggle. My dear, we *always* knew it wasn't Wakefield. You can be assured that if Wakefield were ever to commit murder, it would be much better executed than your mess. Come now. It won't be so bad. Violet won't really be able to bribe the hangman to strangle you instead of breaking your neck."

Gertrude's hand was on her neck again, and she shook her head over and over again. "No! I—No!"

"Let me give you a little hint, my dear," Ham said kindly. "If you want to try to show you were insane and try for an asylum, you have to be a little less calculating and a lot more emotional."

"You don't understand," Gertrude said. "If Barty's secrets got out, my parents would make me break off the engagement. It wasn't easy to find someone they didn't turn away immediately who was *also* controllable. You don't know what it's like to have them watch my every move. It's not *fair!*"

"Just admit to what you did, my dear. Then tell Detective Clarkson pretty lies about how Theo treated you. It's his job to write them all down even if he doesn't believe them."

Gertrude stared at Ham and finally, slowly caved in on herself. The first tear fell and then the second. With a sly glance at Ham, she moaned, "I didn't want to. I didn't want to. He was hurting me. He was *making me* sleep with him. If I didn't..." Gertrude threw herself at Ham, who glanced down at the woman in his arms in utter disgust and shoved her at the ready constable.

"You get all that, Peters?"

"Yes, sir."

"Take her in. I'll be along."

Violet dropped her ginger wine glass, staring at Ham. She hadn't believed, not until Ham turned to her and met her gaze with triumph.

"Did we—" She couldn't finish the sentence.

"We did," Ham agreed. "Jack will be fine now."

Violet gasped and found her heart again. It pounded against her chest so hard it was painful. She pressed her hands into her face and found that the dam could break after all. A watery sob, and Victor was scooping her out of her chair and sitting down with her again.

"There, there," her twin said in that way that spoke so much more. All the things that there weren't words to convey.

Violet pressed her face into his shoulder and sobbed. She couldn't make it stop.

"There, there," Victor said again, rubbing her back like she was a child.

She felt an unfamiliar hand on her head.

"I'll have him there, Vi," Ham promised. "Put on your pretty dress, put flowers in your hair, and find your smiles. That's all he wants."

CHAPTER TWENTY-ONE

"I don't think it would have worked without Clara," Lila said as she pinned Violet's veil in place. "You'll have to send her something amazing for her ready lies. That's when she started to crack. Denny talked about it all night."

Violet didn't want to think on it. Jack hadn't made it back the previous night, but Ham had warned Victor that the interviews with Gertrude would all take too long to believe.

Kate was crying already as she buttoned up the back of Violet's dress. "Growing a baby makes you weepy, Vi. Prepare yourself."

Violet bit down on her lip, thinking of those little spirits that still haunted her. She said nothing, however. Her eyes burned from a night of crying and tossing helplessly, wondering if Jack would come home to her that night. She was pale, her eyes were red-rimmed, her lips were dry from too many tears, but she felt as though she might fly.

She stared into the mirror when she was finished being dressed. It seemed that the long white dress, the veil, the flowers in her hair, the pearls, all of it somehow hid how she'd fallen to pieces and felt too fragile to move. She pinched herself, but it wasn't a dream.

The journey to the church was a blur. The feel of Victor's hand holding her steady was all that she had until he handed her to her father. Violet felt as though she'd stepped into a dream when she walked into the candlelit, flower-strewn chapel.

Jack's back was to her, but she knew those broad shoulders. She hadn't believed they'd make it this far. For what felt like an eternity, she'd been certain that they'd be—at the very least—late for this moment. Her father had to tug her down the aisle, and Violet passed every onlooker without seeing a single face.

Finally, Jack turned, and she drank in the sight of him. He looked as tired as she did, but his eyes...those eyes...they were filled with her, and she could see herself in them. Somehow, she shone.

When her father handed her over to Jack, it was only her beloved's grip on her hands that kept her from floating with joy. She didn't hear anything at all until she heard Jack's name. She snapped back into the moment when the vicar asked, "John Wakefield Junior, will you take Violet Carlyle to be your wife? Will you love her, comfort her, honor and protect her, forsaking all others, and be faithful to her as long as you both shall live?"

"I will," Jack said clearly, and Violet knew that at least one tear had fallen. She suspected it might be a full river of tears.

The vicar was speaking to her then, but Violet had eyes and ears only for Jack. When it was her turn to answer, Jack had to squeeze her hand. She gasped before she said, "I will" and there were a few low chuckles.

Things turned back into a blur until Jack pulled her forward and kissed her gently. He pulled away, and then leaned back towards her, kissing her eyes, her forehead, her cheeks before he looked up at the vicar and nodded.

Tucked into Jack's side with his arm around her shoulders, Vi breathed him in while their friends cheered, and then they rushed down the aisle. When they reached the doors, Jack said, "I changed the plans."

Violet gasped and he lifted her into his arms and rushed down the steps and into a waiting car. "Go!" he commanded the driver.

Violet stared at Jack.

"I thought we'd avoid all the commentary on our last week and the platitudes, and get right to the honeymoon," Jack explained. "Unless you want to go back?"

Vi shook her head, still staring at him, and he wrapped his hand around the back of her and pulled her in for a kiss. "I love you, Violet Wakefield."

Violet smiled against his lips at the sound of her new name. "I love you, Jack Wakefield."

Somehow, between being released from Scotland Yard and the wedding that morning, Jack had arranged a suite at the Hotel Saffron. He took her inside, bypassing everyone but the elevator attendant, who grinned at Violet in her finery and selected the floor without being told.

Jack tugged Violet down the hall. He turned as they entered the suite and backed her against the door as it closed.

She looked up at him through her lashes. "Did we really make it this far, or is it all a dream?"

"We're here. *You* saved me."

"I suppose I owed you one, but you can be my knight-in-distress," Violet told him, grinning wickedly and feeling a rush of joy followed by a rush of nervousness.

Slowly Jack lifted her hand to his face and kissed her on the palm. He followed with a kiss on each one of her fingertips. Then her forehead. Each cheek and finally her lips. He brought her to a haze of need and—like always—made her feel loved and protected through every moment. As he finally lifted her into his arms, he whispered to her, "This is when the happily ever after starts, my love."

The End

Hullo, my friends, I have so much gratitude for you reading my books. Almost as wonderful as giving me a chance are reviews, and indie folks, like myself, need them desperately! If you wouldn't mind, I would be so grateful for a review.

. . .

The sequel to this book, A Jazzy Little Murder, is available for preorder now.

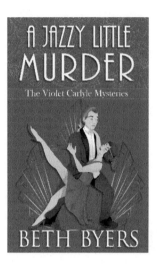

AUGUST 1925.

Violet and Jack have returned home from their honeymoon and are back to their old lives. Jack is taking cases again. Violet is writing books with her twin, managing her business interests, and decorating her house.

When their crew of friends gather for a night on the town, they intend to enjoy cocktails, jazz, and maybe a very late dinner. What they don't expect is one of the band to fall dead while they dance. The celebration comes to a stumbling halt, and the group turns their attention—once again—to why someone would kill a member of the band.

Order Here.

If you enjoy mysteries with a historical twist, scroll to the end for a sample of my new mystery series, The Poison Ink Mysteries. The first book, Death by The Book is available now.

Inspired by classic fiction and Miss Buncle's Book. Death by the Book questions what happens when you throw a murder into idyllic small town England.

July 1936

When Georgette Dorothy Marsh's dividends fall along with the banks, she decides to write a book. Her only hope is to bring her account out of overdraft and possibly buy some hens. The problem is that she has so little imagination she uses her neighbors for inspiration.

She little expects anyone to realize what she's done. So when *Chronicles of Harper's Bend* becomes a bestseller, her neighbors are questing to find out just who this "Joe Johns" is and punish him.

Things escalate beyond what anyone would imagine when one of her prominent characters turns up dead. It seems that the fictional end Georgette had written for the character spurred a real-life murder. Now to find the killer before it is discovered who the author is and she becomes the next victim.

Order Here.

. . .

If you want book updates, you could follow me on Facebook.

DEATH BY THE BOOK PREVIEW

Chapter One

GEORGETTE MARSH

*G*eorgette Dorothy Marsh stared at the statement from her bank with a dawning horror. The dividends had been falling, but this...this wasn't livable. She bit down on the inside of her lip and swallowed frantically. *What was she going to do?* Tears were burning in the back of her eyes, and her heart was racing frantically.

There wasn't enough for—for—anything. Not for cream for her tea or resoling her shoes or firewood for the winter. Georgette glanced out the window, remembered it was spring, and realized that something must be done.

Something, but *what?*

"Miss?" Eunice said from the doorway, "the tea at Mrs. Wilkes is this afternoon. You asked me to remind you."

Georgette nodded, frantically trying to hide her tears from her maid, but the servant had known Georgette since the day of her birth, caring for her from her infancy to the current day.

"What has happened?"

"The...the dividends," Georgette breathed. She didn't have enough air to speak clearly. "The dividends. It's not enough."

Eunice's head cocked as she examined her mistress and then she said, "Something must be done."

"But what?" Georgette asked, biting down on her lip again. *Hard.*

CHARLES AARON

"Uncle?"

Charles Aaron glanced up from the stack of papers on his desk at his nephew some weeks after Georgette Marsh had written her book in a fury of desperation. It was Robert Aaron who had discovered the book, and it was Charles Aaron who would give it life.

Robert had been working at Aaron & Luther Publishing House for a year before Georgette's book appeared in the mail, and he read the slush pile of books that were submitted by new authors before either of the partners stepped in. It was an excellent rewarding work when you found that one book that separated itself from the pile, and Robert got that thrill of excitement every time he found a book that had a touch of *something*. It was the very feeling that had Charles himself pursuing a career in publishing and eventually creating his own firm.

It didn't seem to matter that Charles had his long history of discovering authors and their books. Familiarity had most definitely *not* led to contempt. He was, he had to admit, in love with reading—fiction especially—and the creative mind. He had learned that some of the books he found would speak only to him.

Often, however, some he loved would become best sellers. With the best sellers, Charles felt he was sharing a delightful secret with the world. There was magic in discovering a new writer. A contagious sort of magic that had infected Robert. There was nothing that Charles enjoyed more than hearing someone recommend a book he'd published to another.

"You've found something?"

Robert shrugged, but he also handed the manuscript over a smile right on the edge of his lips and shining eyes that flicked to the manuscript over and over again. "Yes, I think so." He wasn't confident enough yet to feel certain, but Charles had noticed for some time that Robert was getting closer and closer to no longer needing anyone to guide him.

"I'll look it over soon."

It was the end of the day and Charles had a headache building behind his eyes. He always did on the days when he had to deal with the bestseller Thomas Spencer. He was too successful for his own good and expected any publishing company to bend entirely to his will.

Robert watched Charles load the manuscript into his satchel, bouncing just a little before he pulled back and cleared his throat. The boy—man, Charles supposed—smoothed his suit, flashed a grin, and left the office. Leaving for the day wasn't a bad plan. He took his satchel and—as usual—had dinner at his club before retiring to a corner of the room with an overstuffed armchair, an Old-Fashioned, and his pipe.

Charles glanced around the club, noting the other regulars. Most of them were bachelors who found it easier to eat at the club than to employ a cook. Every once in a while there was a family man who'd escaped the house for an evening with the gents, but for the most part —it was bachelors like himself.

When Charles opened the neat pages of 'Joseph Jones's *The Chronicles of Harper's Bend,* he intended to read only a small portion of the book. To get a feel for what Robert had seen and perhaps determine whether it was worth a more thorough look. After a few pages, Charles decided upon just a few more. A few more pages after that, and he left his club to return home and finish the book by his own fire.

It might have been early summer, but they were also in the middle of a ferocious storm. Charles preferred the crackle of fire wherever possible when he read, as well as a good cup of tea. There was no question that the book was well done. There was no question that Charles would be contacting the author and making an offer on the book. *The Chronicles of Harper's Bend* was, in fact, so captivating in its honesty, he couldn't quite decide whether this author loved the small towns of England or despised them. He rather felt it might be both.

Either way, it was quietly sarcastic and so true to the little village that raised Charles Aaron that he felt he might turn the page and discover the old woman who'd lived next door to his parents or the vicar of the church he'd attended as a boy. Charles felt as though he knew the people stepping off the pages.

Yes, Charles thought, yes. This one, he thought, *this* would be a best seller. Charles could feel it in his bones. He tapped out his pipe into the ashtray. This would be one of those books he looked back on with pride at having been the first to know that this book was the next big thing. Despite the lateness of the hour, Charles approached his bedroom with an energized delight. A letter would be going out in the morning.

~

GEORGETTE MARSH

It was on the very night that Charles read the *Chronicles* that Miss Georgette Dorothy Marsh paced, once again, in front of her fireplace. The wind whipped through the town of Bard's Crook sending a flurry of leaves swirling around the graves in the small churchyard and then shooing them down to a small lane off of High Street where the elderly Mrs. Henry Parker had been awake for some time. She had woken worried over her granddaughter who was recovering too slowly from the measles.

The wind rushed through the cottages at the end of the lane, causing the gate at the Wilkes house to rattle. Dr. Wilkes and his wife were curled up together in their bed sharing warmth in the face of the changing weather. A couple much in love, snuggling into their beds on a windy evening was a joy for them both.

The leaves settled into a pile in the corner of the picket fence right at the very last cottage on that lane of Miss Georgette Dorothy Marsh. Throughout most of Bard's Crook, people were sleeping. Their hot water bottles were at the ends of their beds, their blankets were piled high, and they went to bed prepared for another day. The unseasonable chill had more than one household enjoying a warm cup of milk at bedtime, though not Miss Marsh's economizing household.

Miss Marsh, unlike the others, was not asleep. She didn't have a fire as she was quite at the end of her income and every adjustment must be made. If she were going to be honest with herself, and she very much didn't want to be—she was past the end of her income. Her account had become overdraft, her dividends had dried up, and it might be time to recognize that her last-ditch effort of writing a book about her neighbors had not been successful.

She had looked at the lives of folks like Anthony Trollope who both worked and wrote novels and Louisa May Alcott who wrote to relieve the stress of her life and to help bring in financial help. As much as Georgette loved to read, and she did, she loved the idea that somewhere out there an author was using their art to restart their lives. There was a romance to being a writer, but she wondered just how many writers were pragmatic behind the fairytales they crafted. It wasn't, Georgette thought, going to be her story like Louisa May Alcott. Georgette was going to do something else.

"Miss Georgie," Eunice said, "I can hear you. You'll catch something dreadful if you don't sleep." The sound of muttering chased Georgie, who had little doubt Eunice was complaining about catching something dreadful herself.

"I'm sorry, Eunice," Georgie called. "I—" Georgie opened the door to her bedroom and faced the woman. She had worked for Mr. and Mrs. Marsh when Georgie had been born and in all the years of loss and change, Eunice had never left Georgie. Even now when the economies made them both uncomfortable. "Perhaps—"

"It'll be all right in the end, Miss Georgie. Now to bed with you."

Georgette did not, however, go to bed. Instead, she pulled out her pen and paper and listed all of the things she might do to further economize. They had a kitchen garden already, and it provided the vast majority of what they ate. They did their own mending and did not buy new clothes. They had one goat that they milked and made their own cheese. Though Georgette had to recognize that she rather feared goats. They were, of all creatures, devils. They would just randomly knock one over.

Georgie shivered and refused to consider further goats. Perhaps she could tutor someone? She thought about those she knew and realized that no one in Bard's Crook would hire the quiet Georgette Dorothy Marsh to influence their children. The village's wallflower and cipher? Hardly a legitimate option for any caring parent. Georgette was all too aware of what her neighbors thought of her. She rose again, pacing more quietly as she considered and rejected her options.

Georgie paced until quite late and then sat down with her pen and paper and wondered if she should try again with her writing. Something else. Something with more imagination. She had started her book with fits until she'd landed on practicing writing by describing an episode of her village. It had grown into something more, something beyond Bard's Crook with just conclusions to the lives she saw around her.

When she'd started *The Chronicles of Harper's Bend,* she had been more desperate than desirous of a career in writing. Once again, she recognized that she must do something and she wasn't well-suited to anything but writing. There were no typist jobs in Bard's Crook, no secretarial work. The time when rich men paid for companions for their wives or elderly mothers was over, and the whole of the world was struggling to survive, Georgette included.

She'd thought of going to London for work, but if she left her snug little cottage, she'd have to pay for lodging elsewhere. Georgie sighed into her palm and then went to bed. There was little else to do at that moment. Something, however, must be done.

DEATH BY THE BOOK PREVIEW

Chapter Two

GEORGETTE MARSH

*T*hree days later, the day dawned with a return to summer, and the hills were rolling out from Bard's Crook as though being whispered over by the gods themselves. It seemed all too possible that Aurora had descended from Olympus to smile on the village. Miss Marsh's solitary hen with her cold, hard eyes was click-clacking around the garden, eating her seeds, and generally disgusting the lady of the house.

Miss Marsh had woken to the sound of newspaper boy arriving, but she had dressed rather leisurely. There was little to look forward to outside of a good cup of tea, light on the sugar, and without cream. She told herself she preferred her tea without cream, but in the quiet of her bedroom, she could admit that she very much wanted cream in her tea. If Georgie could persuade a god to her door, it would be the goddess Fortuna to bless Georgie's book and provide enough ready money to afford cream and better teas. Was her life even worth living with the watered-down muck she'd been forced to drink lately?

Georgette put on her dress, which had been old when it had been given to her and was the perfect personification of dowdiness. She might also add to her dream list, enough money for a dress or two. By Jove, she thought, how wonderful would a hat be? A lovely new one? Or perhaps a coat that fit her? The list of things that needed to be replaced in her life was near endless.

She sighed into the mirror glancing over her familiar face with little emotion. She neither liked nor disliked her face. She knew her hair was pretty enough though it tended towards a frizziness she'd never learned to anticipate or tame. The color was a decent medium brown with corresponding medium brown eyes. Her skin was clear of blemishes, for which she was grateful, though she despised the freckles that sprinkled over her nose and cheeks. Her dress rose to her collar, but her freckles continued down her arms and over her chest. At least her lips were perfectly adequate, neither thin nor full, but nothing to cause a second glance. Like all of her, she thought, there was nothing to cause a second glance.

Despite her lackluster looks, she didn't despise her face. She rather liked herself. Unlike many she knew, the inside of her head was not a terrible place to be. She had no major regrets and enjoyed her own humor well enough even if she rarely bothered to share her thoughts with others.

Georgette supposed if she had been blessed with liveliness, she might be rather pretty, but she knew herself well. She was quiet. Both in her persona and voice, and she was easily ignored. It had never been something that she bemoaned. She was who she was and though very few knew her well, those who knew her liked her. Those who knew her well—the very few who could claim such a status—liked her very well.

On a morning when Georgie was not worrying over her bank account, she could be counted on entering the dining room at 9:00 a.m. On that morning, however, she was rather late. She had considered goats again as she brushed her teeth—no one else in Bard's Crook kept goats though there were several who kept cows. Those bedamned goats kept coming back to her mind, but she'd rather sell everything she owned and throw herself on the mercy of the city than keep goats. She had considered trying to sew clothing while she'd pulled on her stockings and slipped her shoes on her feet. She had considered whether she might make hats when she'd brushed her hair, and she had wondered if she might take a lodger as she'd straightened her dress and exited her bedroom.

All of her options were rejected before she reached the base of her stairs, and she entered the dining room with an edge of desperation. As she took her seat at the head of the table and added a very small amount of sugar to her weak tea, her attention was caught by the most unexpected of sights. A letter to the left of her plate. Georgette lifted it with shaking hands and read the return address. Aaron & Luther Publishing. She gasped and then slowly blew out the air.

"Be brave, dear girl," she whispered, as she cut open the envelope. "If they say no, you can always send your book to Anderson Books. Hope is not gone. Not yet."

She pulled the single sheet of paper out and wondered if it was a good sign or a bad sign that they had not returned her book. Slowly, carefully, she unfolded the letter, her tea and toast entirely abandoned as she read the contents.

Moments later, the letter fluttered down to her plate and she sipped her scalding hot tea and didn't notice the burn.

"Is all well, Miss Georgie?" The maid was standing in the doorway. Her wrinkled face was fixated on her girl with the same tense anticipation that had Georgette reading her letter over and over while it lay open on her plate. Those dark eyes were fixated on Georgette's face with careful concern.

"I need cream, Eunice." Georgette nodded to her maid. "We're saved. They want *Chronicles*. My goodness, my *dear, wonderful* woman, see to the cream and let's stop making such weak tea until we discover the details of the fiscal benefits."

Eunice had to have been as relieved as Georgette, but the maid simply nodded stalwartly and came back into the dining room a few minutes later with a fresh pot of strong tea, a full bowl of sugar, and the cream that had been intended for supper. It was still the cheapest tea that was sold in Bard's Crook, but it was black and strong and tasted rather like nirvana on her tongue when Georgette drank it down.

"I'll go up to London tomorrow. He wants to see me in the after-noon, but he states very clearly he wants the book. We're saved."

"Don't count your chickens before they hatch, Miss Georgie."

"By Jove, we aren't just saved from a lack of cream, Eunice. We're saved from goats! We're saved my dear. Have a seat and enjoy a cuppa yourself."

Eunice clucked and returned to the kitchen instead. They might be saved, but the drawing room still needed to be done, dinner still needed to be started, and the laundry and mending were waiting for no woman.

When Miss Marsh made her way into London the following day, she was wearing her old cloche, which was quite dingy but the best she had, a coat that was worn at the cuffs and the hem, and shoes that were just starting to have a hole worn into the bottom. Perhaps, she thought, there would even be enough to re-sole her shoes.

On the train into London from Bard's Crook, only Mr. Thornton was taking the train from the village. When he inquired after her busi-ness, she quite shocked herself when she made up a story about meeting an old Scottish school chum for tea. Mr. Thornton admitted he intended to meet with his lawyer. He was rather notorious in Bard's Crook for changing his will as often as the wind changed direction. An event he always announced with an air of doom and a frantic waggling of his eyebrows.

Mr. Thornton had married a woman from the factories who refused to acknowledge her past, and together they had three children. Those children—now adults—included two rebellious sons and one clinging daughter. He also had quite a slew of righteous nephews who deserved the acclaim they received. Whenever his wife bullied him too hard or his sons rebelled too overtly, the will altered in favor of the righteous nephews until such time as an appropriate repentance could be made.

Georgie had long since taken to watching the flip-flopping of the will with a delighted air. As far as she could tell, no one but herself enjoyed the changing of his will, but enjoying things that others didn't seem to notice had long been her fate.

The fortunate news of the inheritance situation was that Mr. Thornton's nephews were unaware of the changing of their fortunes. The clinging daughter's fortune was set in stone. She never rebelled and thus never had her fortunes reversed, but she clung rather too fiercely to be a favored inheritor.

Mr. Thornton handed Miss Marsh down from the train, offered to share a black cab, and then left her without regret when she made a weak excuse. Miss Marsh selected her own black cab, cutting into her ready money dreadfully, and hoped that whatever occurred today would restore her cash in hand.

∼

CHARLES AARON

"Mr. Aaron," Schmidt said, "your afternoon appointment has arrived."

"Wonderful," Charles replied. "Send him in with tea, will you Schmidtty?"

"Her, sir."

"Her? Isn't my appointment with an author?" Charles felt a flash of irritation. He was very much looking forward to meeting the author of *The Chronicles of Harper's Bend*. He had, in fact, read the book twice more since that first time.

Schmidt's lips twitched when he said, "It seems the author is a Miss Marsh."

Charles thought over the book and realized that of course Mr. Jones was a Miss Marsh. Who but a woman would realize the fierce shame of bribing one's children with candies to behave for church? Charles could almost hear the tirade of his grandmother about the lack of mothering skills in the upcoming generations.

"Well, send her in, and tea as well." Charles rubbed his hands together in glee. He did adore meeting new writers. They were never what you expected, but they all had one thing in common. Behind their dull or beautiful faces, behind their polite smiles and small talk, there were whole worlds. Characters with secrets that only the writer knew. Unnecessary histories that were cut viciously from the story and hidden away only to be known by the author.

Charles rather enjoyed asking the writers random questions about their characters' secret histories. Tell me, author, Charles would say, as they shared a cup of tea or a pipe, what does so-and-so do on Christmas morning? Or what is his/her favorite color? He loved when they answered readily, knowing that of course so-and-so woke early on Christmas morning, opened presents and had a rather spectacular full English only to sleep it off on the Chesterfield near the fire.

He loved it when they described what they ate down to the nearest detail as though the character's traditional breakfast had been made since time immemorial rather than born with a pen and hidden behind the gaze of the person with whom Charles was sharing an hour or two.

Charles had long since become inured to the varying attitudes of authors. Thomas Spencer, who had given Charles a rather terrible headache that had been cured by Miss Marsh's delightful book, wore dandified clothes and had an arrogant air. Spencer felt the cleverness of his books justified his rudeness.

On the other hand, an even more brilliant writer, Henry Moore, was a little man with a large stomach. He kept a half-dozen cats, spoiled his children terribly, and was utterly devoted to his wife. In a gathering of authors, Moore would be the most successful and the cleverest by far but be overshadowed by every other writer in attendance.

Miss Marsh, Charles saw, fell into the 'Moore' category. She seemed as timid as a newborn rabbit as she edged into his office. Her gaze flit about, taking in the stack of manuscripts, the shelf of books he'd published over the course of his career, the windows that looked onto a dingy alleyway, and the large wooden desk.

She was, he thought, a dowdy little thing. Her eyes were nice enough, but they barely met his own, and she didn't seem to know quite what to say. Her freckles seemed to be rather spectacular—if one liked freckles—but it was hard to anything with her timid movements. Especially with her face barely meeting his own. That was all right, he thought, he'd done this many times, and she was very new to the selling of a book and the signing of contracts.

"Hello," he said rather cheerily, hoping that his tone would set her at ease.

She glanced up at him and then back down, her gaze darting around his office again. Mr. Aaron wondered just what she was seeing amidst all of his things. He wouldn't be surprised to find she was noting things that the average fellow would overlook.

"Would you like tea?"

Miss Marsh nodded, and he poured her a cup to which she added a hefty amount of cream and sugar. He grinned at the sight of her milky tea and then leaned back as she slowly spun her teacup on the saucer.

"Why Joseph Jones? Why a pen name at all?"

Miss Marsh blinked rather rapidly and then admitted, "Well..." Her gaze darted to the side, and she said, "I was rather inspired by my neighbors, but I would prefer to avoid their gossip as well. Can you imagine?" A cheeky grin crossed her face for a moment, and he was entranced. "If they discovered that Antoinette Moore wrote a book?"

"Is that you?"

"Pieces of her," she admitted, and he frowned. The quiet woman in front of him certainly had the mannerisms of the character, but he couldn't quite see Miss Moore writing a book and sending it off. She was such an innocuous, almost unnecessary character in the book.

Was Miss Marsh was a literary portraitist? He grinned at the idea and wanted nothing more than to visit Harper's Bend or wherever it was that this realistic portrayal existed in real life. What he would give to have an afternoon tea with the likes of Mrs. Morton and her ilk.

Mr. Aaron glanced over Miss Marsh. Her old cloche and worn coat were not lost on him, and he supposed if he'd met her anywhere else he'd never have looked at her twice. Having read her book, however, he suddenly felt as though she were far more charming than she'd otherwise have been.

Her gaze, with ordinary medium brown eyes, seemed to have untold depths, and her freckles seemed to be an outward indicator of a woman who could look at her village and turn it into a witty caricature, acting as a warning that this was a woman who said nothing and noticed everything.

He grinned at her. "I read your book, and I liked it."

Her eyes flashed and a bright grin crossed her face, and he realized she was a little prettier than he'd noticed. It was that shocked delight on her face that made him add, "I like it quite well indeed."

Miss Marsh clasped her hands tightly together, and Mr. Aaron did not miss how her grip camouflaged the trembling of her hands.

"Tell me about it," he said kindly. "Why did you write it? This is a portrait of your neighbors?"

It was the kindness that got Miss Marsh to open up, and then she couldn't seem to stem the tide of her thoughts; they sped out. "Well, it was my dividends you see. They've quite dried up. I was struggling before, but they'd always come in and then they didn't, and I was quite —" Miss Marsh trailed off and Mr. Aaron could imagine the situation all too easily. "at my wit's end. Only then I thought of Louisa May Alcott and the other lady writers, and I thought I might as well try as not."

The world was struggling and Miss Marsh, who may have escaped the early failing of things, had eventually succumbed as so many had. As she said, her dividends had dried up. He could imagine her lying awake worried and uncertain or perhaps pacing her home. There was something so unpretentious about her revelation that Mr. Aaron was even more charmed. She'd come to the end of things, and she'd turned that worry into the most charming of stories. Not just a charming story, but one filled with heart and delight in the little things. He liked her all the better for it.

ALSO BY BETH BYERS

Cookies & Catastrophe

Poison & Pie

Double Mocha Murder

Cinnamon Rolls & Cyanide

Tea & Temptation

Donuts & Danger

Scones & Scandal

Lemonade & Loathing

Wedding Cake & Woe

Honeymoons & Honeydew

The Pumpkin Problem

ALSO BY AMANDA A. ALLEN

The Mystic Cove Mommy Mysteries

Bedtimes & Broomsticks

Runes & Roller Skates

Banshees and Babysitters

Hobgoblins and Homework

Christmas and Curses

Valentines & Valkyries

The Rue Hallow Mysteries

Hallow Graves

Hungry Graves

Lonely Graves

Sisters and Graves

Yule Graves

Fated Graves

Ruby Graves

The Inept Witches Mysteries

(co-written with Auburn Seal)

Inconvenient Murder

Moonlight Murder

Bewitched Murder

Presidium Vignettes (with Rue Hallow)

Prague Murder

Paris Murder

Murder By Degrees

50733313R00106

Made in the USA
Middletown, DE
27 June 2019